LOVE ON ICE

Dr Becky Hope's estranged husband is dying in a hospice, his mistress at his bedside. Distraught and exhausted, Becky turns to her colleague Dr Jake Lachlan, who at first is unaware that she's married. When he does find out, wanting to put some space between them, he joins an Antarctic expedition as a ship's medic — unaware that Becky is the second doctor. Although they try to avoid each other, dramatic events on board bring them unavoidably together . . .

TERESA ASHBY

LOVE ON ICE

Complete and Unabridged

LINFORD
Leicester

First published in Great Britain in 2009

First Linford Edition
published 2011

British Library CIP Data

Ashby, Teresa.
  Love on ice. - -
  (Linford romance library)
  1. Ship physicians- -Fiction.
  2. Love stories.
  3. Large type books.
  I. Title II. Series
  823.9'2–dc22

  ISBN 978–1–44480–602–1

Published by
F. A. Thorpe (Publishing)
Anstey, Leicestershire

Set by Words & Graphics Ltd.
Anstey, Leicestershire
Printed and bound in Great Britain by
T. J. International Ltd., Padstow, Cornwall

This book is printed on acid-free paper

1

Becky Hope pushed back the sheets and reached for Jake's robe. It felt cool against her burning skin and it smelled like he had last night, fresh from the shower. Jake smiled down at her and placed a cup of coffee on the bedside table, but she didn't return his smile.

'Becky . . . ?' Was that uncertainty in his voice?

She straightened her shoulders and drew in a deep breath to compose herself into the tough, good time girl she must pretend to be.

'About last night, Jake,' she said flippantly. 'I was drunk, end of story.'

She was shaken by the shock she saw reflected briefly in his eyes and had to avert her gaze. Such beautiful eyes. Eyes that had reminded her of lapis lazuli from the moment she first saw him. Stunningly blue and sparking with gold fire.

'You're kidding, right?' Jake said, puzzled. 'What's going on?'

This had to count as the worst thing she'd ever done in her entire life, the lowest possible thing that she'd ever managed to stoop to.

'Becky?' He reached out for her and she moved swiftly out of reach.

'Don't,' she said, that one word sounding so cold and final even to her own ears. She put up her hand as if to ward him off. 'Don't touch me. Last night meant nothing. The sooner you accept that, the better for both of us.'

He was quick to recover, just as she hoped he'd be and his eyebrows rose mockingly.

'Wow,' he murmured. 'You believe in telling it like it is, don't you?'

But the way he avoided looking at her while running his fingers through his tousled blonde hair was a dead give-away. A lock fell over his eyes and he brushed it back impatiently. For a moment he'd looked vulnerable.

'I don't really understand what your problem is,' she said, trying to avoid his eyes. 'I thought you'd be happy with the no-strings approach. That's what guys like you are all about isn't it?'

'Guys like me?' he said. 'You seriously think that's what I've been about the past few weeks? Do you really think all I was interested in was a one-night stand?'

'Well, given your reputation . . . ' she began only to be slashed by a deadly look from him.

'My reputation?'

'Around the hospital,' her voice was weakening.

'You assumed by listening to gossip that I was up for a good time and nothing more, right?' he rapped out the words.

'You got what you wanted,' she said harshly.

'I wouldn't say that,' he said.

Becky tried hard not to look at him.

'You really are something else,

Becky,' he said and it didn't sound like a compliment, in fact his voice was thick with a loathing that made her stomach contract painfully.

'Aren't I just?' she responded harshly, trying to live up to this new image she'd been forced to create for herself.

'You come from nowhere, act like you might just like me, then last night you knock on my door and throw yourself at me. I should have asked why the sudden change of heart instead of just assuming my luck had changed.'

He shook his head and took a step away from her.

'I'll just use your shower if I may, then I'll be getting off.'

'Sure, help yourself. You seem to pretty much do that anyway.'

'Oh, come on,' Becky fired back, stung. 'You weren't exactly fighting me off! What's wrong with you, Jake? Your masculine pride dented, is it?'

'Yeah,' he said. 'If you want to look at it like that, then fine, that's exactly how it is. I just don't get how you could be all over me last night and then this morning you're turning the cold shoulder.'

She turned away and he crossed the bedroom and caught her by her shoulders, spinning her round to face him, searching her eyes with his.

'What's going on with you, Becky?'

He managed to look angry and despairing all at the same time and her heart wept for him.

All she had left was the truth. Or at least part of it.

'I'm married,' she said flatly.

'Married?' he gasped, even more shocked than he had been before. 'You don't wear a ring.'

'It's impractical at work,' she said.

He looked as if he'd been hit.

'Married,' he said again, disbelief thickening his voice. 'Why didn't you say something sooner? Why let me go on thinking I was in with a chance? How can you keep something like a husband quiet?'

'I didn't intend to,' she said.

'There are names for women like you,' he said softly. 'Go on, have your shower. And then get out.'

★   ★   ★

If only it were as easy to get her out of his life as it was to throw her out of his apartment, he thought, pacing the kitchen as he waited impatiently for her to leave.

She'd fallen asleep in his arms, he'd assumed with drink and exhaustion, and he'd carried her to his bed. It had taken every ounce of willpower he possessed to leave her there.

If she hadn't fallen asleep . . .

If he'd thought for one minute. He still couldn't believe he'd let her draw him in like that. Okay, he'd wanted her from the moment she first set foot in the hospital, but she could have told him at the outset that she was married.

She'd let him make a complete idiot of himself. Building up to asking her out, taking things easy at first. A coffee at the café opposite the hospital, a drink or two in the bar after shift. Slowly building up a friendship that had led to last night when he actually thought that for once in his life, he might have got things right.

But instead he'd got things wrong. He couldn't have got them more wrong. He'd fallen for a woman like that once before in his life and he'd just about managed to convince himself that his ex-wife wasn't typical of her breed when along came Becky to shatter his illusions.

She'd always seemed vulnerable somehow, not in the least worldly wise. It was that vulnerability that had first drawn him to her.

Thalia had found it easy to cheat on him, or so it seemed. Their marriage had lasted nine months, the length of a pregnancy and at the end of the gestation period had given birth to a whole lot of bitterness and grief.

With Becky he'd been ready for a proper full-on relationship again and he'd been so sure that she was the one.

How about that for completely lousy judgement?

She'd arrived out of nowhere on a temporary contract at the hospital and he'd fallen for her.

He heard footsteps coming from the bedroom. He'd never run away from anything in his life, but working with her after this was going to be impossible. How could you work with someone you wanted so desperately and hated so much? Except he couldn't bring himself to hate her.

He went out to the hall. She looked small, diminished, her eyes almost sunken with sadness. Never forget, he reminded himself, she has a husband at home waiting for her.

She hesitated briefly as if she wanted to say something.

'Just go,' he said and turned away.

He thought about the hospital, working with her every day, the torture of seeing her and knew he couldn't do it. There was only one thing left to do and oddly enough, she was the only person he'd discussed it with. When he'd told her about the job offer from an old friend her violet eyes had lit up.

They'd been having a coffee after work, sitting at an outside table enjoying the evening sunshine.

'Medic on an Antarctic expedition? You lucky thing,' she'd said without hesitation. 'You'd be mad to pass up a chance like that. On an ice breaker too! How fantastic!'

'Would you?' he'd asked, amazed that she hadn't shuddered and said he'd be crazy to take it. 'Give up everything and take off, just like that?'

'I'd jump at a chance like that,' she said eagerly. 'I went as a medic on an Arctic expedition last year. It was the most incredible and amazing experience of my entire life.'

'It's not that easy,' he'd said. 'I'm pretty well settled at the hospital and it would be too much to expect them to keep my job open. This is where my home is, where my friends are, and I know it sounds boring, but probably

9

where my future lies. I can't throw all that away for a few weeks adventure.'

'I can see why you wouldn't,' she'd smiled at him. There was another reason for turning down the job and she was sitting right opposite him, captivating him with her beautiful eyes.

'I've done a few trips down south,' he said.

'But you're not tempted to go again?' she said. 'Not even a little bit.'

'Not in the slightest,' he said. 'I'm one hundred per cent committed to my life here now.'

And at the time he'd meant it. Every word.

When he heard the front door click quietly shut behind her, he picked up the phone with a heavy heart.

'Alex?' he said. 'Hi, it's Jake.'

'Jake! Good to hear from you,' Alex said cheerfully. 'How're you doing?'

'Fine,' Jake said. 'Look. I'll get straight to the point. That job we talked about. Is it still open?'

They'd been at university together,

sharing digs, but their lives had taken very different directions. Alex was a marine biologist.

Jake didn't know much about krill and the movement and thickness of ice floes. He didn't understand the significance of numbers of penguins, whales and seals in the grand scheme of things, but it didn't matter. He'd be along as medical back up to the team. All he had to do was take care of the crew's health.

'You're serious? You'll come? That's fantastic, Jake. We'll get together soon and go over the finer details.'

How about that? He was literally going to the ends of the earth to escape his humiliation at the hands of Becky Hope.

'You know we leave in three weeks? Can you get away that quickly?'

'I can,' Jake said, swallowing the lump in his throat. He was burning his boats. There could be no going back.

'I can't tell you how pleased I am about this,' Alex said. 'You wouldn't believe the trouble we've had finding suitably qualified doctors for this expedition. There are plenty who are keen and willing, but finding those with the proper survival skills and level of experience is like looking for the proverbial needle in a haystack.'

'I can imagine,' Jake said. 'I've screened candidates for some of these trips myself and it's a tough business.'

'So why the sudden change of heart — or shouldn't I ask?' Alex said.

'Personal reasons,' Jake replied abruptly.

'Subject to you passing the medical, you're on the team,' Alex said, changing the subject.

'I already did,' Jake reminded him. 'When I did those Southern Ocean trips with you in the past.'

'That was some time ago, Jake,' Alex said. 'I know you have all the skills necessary for this trip. I just want to be absolutely certain you're medically fit for it. You're up to scratch on all your survival techniques?'

'Absolutely,' Jake said, then added dryly. 'You know me, Alex. I'm the world's greatest survivor.'

2

Becky pulled up in the quiet hospice car park and rested her forehead on the steering wheel, unable to halt the tears any longer. Oh, what a mess! Not just what happened today, but everything, her whole rotten life. Last night had finally brought home to her how shallow and pointless her marriage had been, made her realise that she'd never loved Bryn.

She heard knuckles rapping on the window and looked up, blinking back tears, to see Sister Bernadette looking into the car.

She smiled and rubbed her eyes with the back of her hands, then opened the door and stepped out into fresh air and the full blast of Sister Bernadette's warm sympathy.

'My dear child,' she began and Becky shook her head. A kind word now could be her undoing. Sister Bernadette seemed to understand.

'He had a good night,' Sister Bernadette reported as they turned towards the building. 'Peaceful.' She looked thoughtful for a moment, then with a direct look at Becky added, 'She didn't leave.'

'No,' Becky said. 'Apparently she's decided to stay with him until the end. It's what he wants.'

'I see,' Sister Bernadette sniffed. She knew the situation. Becky had felt it only honest and fair to make it clear to her and she liked it even less than Becky did if that were possible. But her concern was with the dying man in her care and in making his last days on earth as comfortable and peaceful as possible no matter what he'd done.

They walked on in silence, only the swish of Sister Bernadette's crisp, clean habit and the wet gravel crunching underfoot to accompany them. Outside the main door of the old, ivy clad building the nun paused and put her hand on Becky's arm.

'How long have you known?' she asked.

'He was with her when he first collapsed,' Becky said, the tears back in her eyes as she recalled that awful night. 'He'd already left me to go and live with her several weeks before he was taken ill. I'd been away — run away in fact — to the Arctic and I'd only been back a few days when I got the call. It was an acrimonious parting, Sister. We didn't separate on good terms as you can imagine.'

Her chest ached with sadness and her throat burned with the effort of holding back tears.

'But when you found out how ill he was, you took him back?'

'Elizabeth called me out of the blue a few months ago,' she said. 'She said my husband had collapsed in her bathroom and wanted to know what I intended to do about it.'

Sister Bernadette let out a small gasp of shock.

Becky's prime concern then had been for her husband's health. They'd been married for only two years and in the weeks before he left her, he'd been complaining of dizzy spells and headaches. When she'd tried to persuade him to see a doctor, he'd laughed in her face.

'I'll call an ambulance,' she'd told Elizabeth. And then it had occurred to her. She didn't know where Elizabeth lived — didn't even, at that point, know her name. Those details sorted out, she'd made the call and set off for the hospital to be there to greet the ambulance.

Bryn had arrived alone and frightened. Elizabeth had chosen to remain at home. She had abandoned him.

Becky looked at Sister Bernadette through a mist of tears.

'When she found out that he had a brain tumour and would require hospital treatment, Elizabeth bowed out completely. Until last night, I had never even seen her. She hasn't been to visit him once in all this time.'

'How did she know he was here?' Sister Bernadette asked.

'I told her,' Becky said. 'I've kept her informed every step of the way. He asks about her, you see. And every week I phone her up and give her an update on his condition. Last time I called her I told her it wouldn't be long and if she wanted to say goodbye . . . '

She closed her eyes against the wave of pain that admission caused. Although she no longer loved her husband, she'd been through too much with him not to feel something for the man, even it was only pity.

Becky had taken the job at City Hospital for the shorter working hours and the closer proximity to the hospice and there she had met Jake and revelled in the normality of her working day.

She still didn't know why she hadn't told any of her new colleagues about her husband. Perhaps she didn't want their sympathy. Or maybe for a few hours every day she liked to pretend

17

that none of this had happened. She'd gone into denial, in just the same way she'd gone into denial about her husband's relationship with another woman.

And dear Donald her mentor and father figure who had given her the job had gone along with her wishes.

'Fancy a drink after work?' she heard the echo of Jake's voice in her head. An invitation so casually given, so gratefully received.

'Great.' It was just a drink after all. It didn't mean anything.

Oh, when she thought about it, she'd well and truly led him up the garden path, culminating finally in last night. Poor Jake.

'Let me go on ahead and ask her to leave,' Sister Bernadette said now.

Becky smiled, appreciating the nun's thoughtfulness. But she could cope. She'd have to since Elizabeth had suddenly decided that she wanted to play a major part in what remained of Bryn's life.

Her arrival last night had been a shock. Becky had been sitting beside his bed, moistening his lips with a sponge when she'd felt the presence of someone else in the room. She'd never seen Elizabeth, but knew who she was as soon as she saw the shock on her face.

'Is he really dying?' she'd asked.

'This is a hospice,' Becky said coldly. 'I did explain all this to you on the phone. He may not see or talk very well, but he can still hear perfectly.'

'Oh my God,' Elizabeth had taken three unsteady steps towards the bed. 'He looks so ill. What happened to his hair?'

'He is ill,' Becky said, gritting her teeth. She saw no point in going into the details of Bryn's harsh and, in the end, pointless treatment. 'And as I already told you, he can still hear everything.'

And then Elizabeth was peeling off her coat, dropping it over the back of a chair and moving ever closer to Bryn's side. She was every bit the tragic heroine, come to share her lover's last few hours. His eyes didn't exactly light up at the sight of her, but there was a spark of recognition in his dulled eyes and he tried to reach out his hand.

He was very rarely conscious now thanks to the high doses of morphine. His periods of sleep were growing longer and Becky knew it wouldn't be long before he fell into that last deep sleep that would herald the final hours.

He had already entered the active phase of dying.

'I think he wants you to hold his hand,' Becky said.

She felt sick. She'd been here with him through the worst of his illness and now this woman, this ice-cold blonde, had walked in and taken his hand ready to play the tragic lover. Her make up, Becky noticed, was absolutely flawless. 'Have you any idea what he's been through these past few weeks?' Becky said softly. 'What we've both been through?'

But Elizabeth wasn't listening. She was holding his hand, stroking it, murmuring words of love and devotion.

And so she'd left the hospice with what remained of her dignity, stopping by at Sister Bernadette's dimly lit office to tell her that she was leaving.

And she'd driven slowly, carefully towards the docks where she knew Jake Lachlan had an apartment. She'd sat outside looking up at the lights, wanting to run to him, wanting to tell him everything.

But her courage failed her and when she finally got out of her car, she'd walked to the wine bar on the waterfront where she and Jake had had drinks a couple of times. She'd sat alone at the bar nursing glass after glass of red wine and although she wasn't fall down drunk, she was far from sober and she was tired, so tired.

To have driven home in that state would have been downright dangerous, never mind illegal and so she'd made her way, rather unsteadily, to Jake's apartment where she stood for a while before pressing the intercom button.

'It's me, Becky,' was all she'd said and there had been an immediate buzz for the door to open and Jake's sleepy voice saying, 'Come on up.'

He was waiting upstairs, his hair tousled.

She'd woken him.

Her carefully thought out speech in which she would ask him to call a taxi for her was forgotten at the sight of him. The last thing she wanted was to go home. She'd opened her mouth to speak, but no words had come and she'd gone into his arms instead.

He'd held back for a second, then he'd gathered her up in his arms, kicked the door shut behind them and carried her inside. She didn't remember anything at all after that, but she could fill in the gaps. And her face burned with shame.

She pushed away memories of last night and entered the quiet room.

'I want to go home and get changed,'

Elizabeth said as soon as she walked in. 'I've been sitting here all night. I need a rest.'

'Of course you do,' Becky said, struggling to dredge up some kind of sympathy for this woman.

'It's been an ordeal,' Elizabeth added shakily. 'He seems to be unconscious now. I kept thinking he'd stopped breathing . . . '

Becky reached out. She couldn't help herself. It wasn't in her nature to be cruel and she folded her hand around Elizabeth's which felt cold and almost lifeless. The woman did not respond in any way to Becky's touch.

'The end is very near,' Becky murmured. 'It won't be long.'

'I bet you can't wait,' Elizabeth said under her breath and pulled her hand away. Then she turned for the door. 'I'll be back.'

Becky stared after her, stunned. She didn't want Bryn's suffering to continue, but she was hardly eager for his death. She closed her eyes, then moved across to the bed.

Bryn was deeply unconscious now. Perhaps he'd been waiting for Elizabeth to come and say goodbye before finally letting himself go.

His family had already been to say their goodbyes, but they found it too painful to stay for any length of time. That had just left Becky.

When the nurses came in to wash him, she went outside and made a call to Donald to tell him she wouldn't be coming back to work — ever.

'It will be soon,' she said, but she knew she was deceiving herself. The reason she wasn't going back was because she couldn't face Jake.

'Of course,' Donald said. 'Let me know . . .'

Then she returned to sit beside the bed and held Bryn's hand until Elizabeth returned later that day in fresh clothes with her make up perfectly restored to take over.

Bryn died three days later without ever regaining consciousness.

The funeral was sparsely attended. Elizabeth was there as chief mourner, draped from head to toe in black, still managing to look glamorous while all Becky could manage was utterly exhausted. She wore black trousers that were too loose from the weight she'd lost and a slightly crumpled white shirt.

She couldn't even cry. She felt so numb. She'd lost Bryn a long, long time ago and in the end his death had been a blessing. The absence of tears was noted and frowned upon. Elizabeth had no such problems and was crying loudly and lapping up the sympathy as Bryn's family gathered round.

Becky couldn't even muster enough energy to feel slighted when some of Bryn's relations thanked Elizabeth effusively for being with Bryn at the end. Only Donald knew what she had been through these past few months.

'They blame me,' Becky said. 'Bryn's family, I mean. They think I should have seen this coming, that I should have stopped it somehow.'

'Would you like me to talk to them?' Donald offered. 'Bryn was under sentence of death long before he showed any symptoms. I could put the record straight.'

'Bryn's dead. Nothing can change that now. After today I will never see any of them again. Besides, they've lost Bryn, it's enough they have to cope with that and if their anger towards me helps, well . . . ' she shrugged.

'Some of your colleagues at the hospital have asked about you,' Donald said. 'I told them you'd to take emergency leave because of a family crisis.'

She wondered if Jake had been one of those to enquire.

'So what now, Becky? Is there any way I can persuade you to take a permanent post at City? There's still a full time position available in the emergency department.'

Work with Jake? There was no way she could do that.

'You've been so kind, Donald,' she

said. 'But I want to get away. I want to make a fresh start and try to put all this behind me.'

They stopped at the graveside for the short burial service.

She held a yellow rose. Yellow because it was the colour of the flowers she had carried at their wedding. Although it was only a little under three years ago, she'd been so much younger then, so full of dreams and hopes. She'd thought she was in love. She'd thought he loved her. She threaded her wedding ring onto the stem of the rose and dropped it onto the coffin.

She watched it drift down and bounce slightly as it landed, then she turned into Donald's waiting arms and moved away, turning her back on the Hope family forever.

She felt as if she'd closed a door. It was almost as if the last three years hadn't happened at all, as if she'd been a spectator, watching the misery of someone else. She'd learnt to hide her own emotions, quell her own fears and somewhere during that time, she'd learnt to harden her heart.

'So what next for Becky Hope?' Donald asked.

'Becky Hope is dead,' she said. 'I'm going back to using my maiden name. New start, old name.'

3

The Delphinus, a rugged ice-breaker research vessel, was surprisingly cosy and it seemed to Jake that they'd been waiting at King George Island forever. When Jake first arrived at Ushuaia in Argentina to join Alex, it was to find that the second doctor on the expedition had not been able to make it after all. Not only that, their sailing had been delayed because of horrendous weather conditions across the Drake Passage.

'Sorry about the delays,' Alex said as he accompanied Jake to his cabin. 'We can't help the weather, but we could have chosen someone more reliable as the second doctor.'

'So what happens now?' Jake asked, his eyes flitting round the small cabin. It was just what he needed. An uncluttered life. Time to gather his thoughts. And where better than on the Antarctic ice?

'It left us in a spot, Jake, I don't mind telling you,' Alex said. 'Not only invalidates all our insurance only having one medic along, but also puts the team and this whole expedition at risk. You know the dangers we face. As soon as the weather clears, we're heading for King George Island and I've arranged to meet our replacement doctor there.'

Alex grinned from behind the black bushy beard he'd grown for this trip.

'Anyway, you're here! That's the main thing,' he said, giving Jake a hearty slap on the shoulder. 'I can't tell you how good it is to see you.'

There was a moment of reflective silence and Jake said, 'So, you've found someone already?'

'Yep. Why? You're not going to tell me you know someone who'd be ideal for the job are you?'

Jake considered for a moment and shook his head. There was only one person he could think of to be second doctor and he would have felt duty bound to put her name forward if Alex had been stuck.

But to suggest Becky Hope for this expedition would be nothing short of madness. If he'd felt unable to work with her within the confines of a hospital, how much more ridiculous would the situation be with them stuck in the Antarctic for months on end with no escape from each other?

Besides, she was married. She wouldn't want to leave her husband behind. The memory of her words when she'd told him she had a husband never failed to stir up a whole maelstrom of emotions. Everything from anger to humiliation mixed in with a good helping of hurt feelings.

He had been grateful for her sudden disappearance, which Donald had apparently believed to be over a family crisis, but there was always the risk that she might come back. Donald was keeping her job open which, as far as Jake was concerned, was a Sword of

Damocles hanging over his head.

'We had a few last minute applications before we left and Dick in London sifted through them until he found someone suitable, which thank god he did. She's perfect. As long as the paperwork can be sorted out, she'll be leaving England as soon as possible and will pick up a plane from Punta Arenas to Frei station to meet us there,' Alex said. 'You just pipped her to the job before we left, but Dick hung on to her application because she was good back up. He's done all the necessary and she's ideal.'

'She?' Jake said. 'Does she have a name?'

'Callaghan,' Alex said and it was all Jake could do not to let out an enormous sigh of relief. For one terrible moment there, he'd thought . . . But no, that would be impossible. Fate couldn't possibly deal such a cruel blow.

'You have a problem with that?' Alex grinned. 'Anyway, from what I've heard this one doesn't mind roughing it. She went on a polar expedition with Des Harrington. Remember Des?'

'Vaguely,' Jake said distractedly. A woman. That's all he needed when he'd come so far to get away from them! But at least it wasn't the woman he was specifically trying to get away from, which was some consolation.

If he ever saw Becky Hope again it would be too soon as far as he was concerned. And if he ever stopped thinking about her it would be nothing short of a miracle. He might have come to the ends of the earth to get away from her, but he couldn't erase her from his mind so easily.

'You'll soon see her,' Alex said. 'You can meet her plane in at Frei.'

'No problem,' Jake murmured.

And now the waiting was almost over.

* * *

As flights went, that had been pure evil. It was all Becky could do to stop her legs shaking as she stepped off the plane. She felt as if her stomach was in her boots and she had a pounding headache, but the last thing she wanted to do was appear sickly or weak because now she was off that plane, she was going to have to step aboard a boat. And that churning sea had looked none too welcoming.

Despite her homework, the ice had come as a shock. And this island was only a taste of what was to come when they went further south and reached the Antarctic peninsula. Some of the work was to be carried out in the Weddell Sea on the pack itself.

She felt a thrill of excitement and anticipation run through her. The trip to the Arctic had been the most exhilarating, uplifting experience of her life and the Antarctic, she had been promised, would eclipse even that.

There was only one guy waiting for the plane, a huge bear of a man who saw her and raised his hand in greeting. He had a thick black beard and was tall and powerful looking. Well I might be short, she thought, but I'm strong and I know what I'm doing. And as for grizzly bearded men, it's just something I'm going to have to get used to.

★ ★ ★

I am fine with this, Jake told himself as he watched the twin engine plane descend through a blanket of cloud. Bad weather had meant delays in the flight from Punta Arenas, but now at last she was here and Alex was planning to get under way immediately Dr Callaghan was on board.

It would have been a turbulent ride for the passengers ending with a first sight of stormy seas and endless ice, not to mention a bumpy landing on the rocky airstrip.

As it turned out, she was the only woman on board. He could have picked her out a mile away, stepping off the plane, looking around her in wonder? Or was it trepidation?

He ran his fingers through his beard. The darkness of it was at odds with his fair hair but it kept his face surprisingly warm.

She had her hood up against the biting wind and wore sunglasses to protect her eyes. Her mouth was covered by a red scarf. She looked his way and he raised his hand and she headed in his direction.

'Hi, you must be Dr Callaghan,' he said, holding out his hand.

That voice! As he spoke he raised his sunglasses and she found herself looking into vivid lapis lazuli blue eyes and felt a jolt of pure panic far more shocking than anything she had prepared herself for. Those eyes were smiling now. Was it possible he didn't realise who she was?

He'd hardly be smiling if he knew.

'You are Dr Callaghan?' he said, his voice gruff as he seemed to sense her sudden uncertainty.

She couldn't speak. For two pins she would have turned on her heel and rushed for the plane, begging the pilot to take her back to Chile.

How could he be here?

When Jake had spoken to her about the Antarctic job, he'd said he had decided positively against taking it. In fact he'd been quite adamant about it. His life and future were at City. What had happened to change his mind? Her heart plummeted. Well, wasn't that obvious? It was her! She'd happened. She'd changed his mind, changed his life. She was the reason for him dashing off to the bottom of the world.

And what was he going to do when he realised that the very person he wanted to escape from had followed him here?

They had a job to do and time was slipping away from them rapidly. They needed particular weather conditions and too much delay at this point could mean putting off the whole thing for another year.

But how were they going to cope with working together?

'I'm Jake Lachlan and . . . '

'I know who you are,' Becky mumbled, her voice muffled by her scarf.

'Sorry?' his voice rose in question and he bent slightly, moving his head closer to hers. She hadn't really noticed the wind screaming around her ears until that moment and suddenly the noise seemed to intensify.

'Did you say you knew me?' he asked with that oh, so familiar good humour of his. 'I'm sorry, I don't remember . . . '

So what to do now? Brazen this thing out? How could she keep up the pretence that she was a hard-nosed man-eater for the coming months? It had been hard enough to carry it off in the space of a few minutes.

He straightened up and looked down at her, cocking his head on one side as if he still hadn't quite heard what she'd said. That beard suited him. It made him look even more rugged, even more masculine. The silence stretched and swelled as Becky wondered how on earth she was going to break this to him. In the end, there was only one way to do it.

She looked up at him and lowered her scarf, then she removed her sunglasses. One look into those violet eyes was all it took.

He looked as if he'd seen a ghost. He even backed away from her a couple of steps as if she might be poisonous. The bewilderment and confusion on his face brought their last meeting — or parting — back to her in vivid detail. He couldn't have looked more horrified if he'd been in a crypt and had just uncovered a vampire!

'What is this, Becky?' he hissed, his eyes flashing with fury. 'Are you following me? Are you hell bent on making my life a misery?'

'No. I had no idea you were here. I thought you'd turned this job down.'

'Change of plan,' he growled. 'What are you doing here?'

'Change of plan,' she said, echoing his words. 'I'm sorry, Jake. I swear I had no idea you'd be here. If you want me to, I'll turn around right now and go back home. It's up to you.'

He stared down at her, his beautiful eyes narrowed against the biting wind, but still she could see the anger there. If only he could learn not to hate her. She'd known him at the hospital as a gentle charmer, mad as a bull when roused but for the most part patient and kind.

'I'd like nothing better than to see your backside disappearing up those steps,' he said with a curt nod towards the plane. 'But you go and this whole expedition gets cancelled. Much as it pains me to say this, Becky, you're vital to this trip and I think too much of Alex to let it fall apart just because you . . . we . . . '

He was floundering and her heart went out to him. If only she could say something, do something to make him feel better about all this. He was a kind, gentle man. He didn't really deserve what she had done to him.

'This would be funny if it wasn't so awful,' Becky muttered.

'Yeah,' he said bitterly. 'Look at me. I can't stop laughing.'

'Could we start afresh?' she asked lamely, knowing even as she said it the incredulity her request would earn.

'Oh, sure,' Jake said. 'We'll pretend that nothing happened between us shall we? That'll be just cosy and hey, it'll leave you free to move amongst the crew as you wish won't it?'

His words, delivered with such bitterness and insinuation stung to the core. She was tired, she felt sick, fed up and now she'd been hit squarely between the eyes with the biggest bombshell ever.

'Oh, grow up and deal with it!' she snapped. 'I'm sorry I hurt you, Jake.'

'Hurt me?' He laughed coldly. 'Don't flatter yourself. You're not that important to me.'

'Then what exactly is your problem?'

'I don't like being used,' he said fiercely.

'So it's pride is it?'

His eyes drilled into her and they faced up to each other for several seconds, then his shoulders relaxed and he shook his head.

'You really do have a high opinion of yourself,' he said.

'Let's just get to the ship,' she murmured wearily. 'I'm tired.'

'Well you'd better get used to being tired,' Jake muttered. 'Otherwise you'll be no use to anyone.'

Becky closed her eyes. She had no idea how she was going to get through the next few weeks and months. Then she squared up her shoulders and looked Jake straight in the eye.

If he was having a problem handling it, then it was just that — his problem, not hers.

After all she'd been through a bit of ice was going to be a doddle. As for Jake Lachlan, well if he had a problem that was his tough luck.

★ ★ ★

'I wasn't told about this,' Jake said. 'I just assumed . . . '

'What? That they'd conjure me up a spare cabin out of thin air?' Becky said, too tired to be bothered by it.

He could do without her mockery. He could do without her full stop.

She'd tossed her bag onto the bottom bunk and now she was opening it, taking out various bits and pieces and lining them up along what would double up as desk and dressing table. Her hands shook as she placed things down, but he wasn't going to be fooled by her pretence of vulnerability. Not again.

That slender little neck held up a hard head.

'Just make sure you take as much space as you need,' he said.

'Oh, I will,' she said.

'Ah, that's right, you always take what you want,' he said. It was too good an opportunity to miss, but even as he said it, he regretted it.

This was going to be one long,

painful trip if they were going to spend the whole time sniping at each other. And much as he hated to admit it, she was right. Not only did he have to learn to handle the situation, he'd have to get on and live with it — live with her. And in much closer confines than he felt comfortable with.

'I'm sorry,' he said as she carried on, blindly unpacking her bag.

When she didn't respond, he reached out and touched her arm. She flinched as if he'd struck her. What had he done to make her hate him so much? He withdrew his hand, but then anger bubbled up inside him and he reached out to her again, this time grabbing her arm and forcing her round to look at him.

It shocked him more than it shocked her. And the even bigger shock was the sight of tears shimmering in her eyes, turning the violet to misty mauve.

'What's happening, Becky?' he growled, dropping his hand from her arm and raking it through his beard in frustration. 'What are we doing? We used to be friends.'

Her watery eyes looked too big for her face and tears turned her eyelashes to black spikes. She rubbed them with the back of her hand, angry at their presence.

'I'm tired,' she said by way of explanation. 'That's all. You're right to be angry, Jake, but there's nothing we can do.'

'I know,' he conceded, his voice softening slightly. 'But I'll have a word with some of the other guys. It's just possible that I could squeeze in with someone else and you can have the cabin to yourself.'

She shook her head and moistened her lips, then smiled that gentle, sweet smile that had sucked him in back home.

'I had to sign an agreement before leaving home,' she said. 'There just isn't the cabin space on board for me to have separate quarters. I knew before I left home that I'd have to share with a guy and I didn't have a problem with it. I just didn't know it would be you I'd be sharing with.'

He drew in his breath and said, 'Well, I guess if you don't mind, then I can live with that.'

'How kind of you,' she murmured.

He looked up sharply, but let it go. She'd peeled off her coat and was wearing a woollen sweater underneath. It drowned her, made her look even smaller than she was. She'd lost weight. Had she been ill? And why the name change? Had her marriage failed?

She looked almost frail and he wondered if, despite passing the medical and fitness tests, she was going to be up to this trip, physically.

She held up her wash bag. 'I think I'd like to freshen up,' she said icily.

'You want me to leave?'

'Just go,' she said, turning away from him.

'Dinner is in the mess at six,' he said, brushing past her to get to the door, physical contact impossible to avoid. 'It's the last door on the left.'

46

4

Becky stood looking at the door for several seconds after it closed behind him. Jake Lachlan. She looked at the bunk above hers. Up there. Every night. And when they weren't sleeping on the boat, they'd be in tents on the ice or possibly even spending time at one of the research stations on land.

Jake didn't look as if he'd lost weight or sleep. Tough, rugged and now with that beard on his face, he looked the picture of good health.

In the bathroom, she ran a sink full of hot water. Tears plopped into the water and she laughed at her reflection in the mirror above the sink.

How ironic that they'd both come to Antarctica to escape and had then come face to face with the very person they'd come to escape from! She washed her face and went back to her unpacking.

There was a light tap on the door.

'Come in.'

The guy who walked in had black curly hair and a beard to match. His grey eyes twinkled in greeting as he held out his hand to her.

'Hi, Rebecca,' he said. 'I'm sorry I wasn't around to welcome you on board. I'm Alex.'

'Hi, Alex,' she smiled. 'It's Becky and I'm glad to be here.'

'Not as glad as we are to have you,' he said. 'Thanks to you, we won't have to abort, which not only saves our sponsors a packet, it saves everyone on board a whole heap of time and trouble. And it means our research — important research — isn't put off for another year.'

He was as tall as Jake, but not as broad and there was a slight stoop to his shoulders as if he was used to walking round bent over in small spaces.

'Settling in okay?' he asked, 'Jake give you the guided tour?'

'Actually, no,' she said.

'He didn't? There's not a lot to see. Just the mess room where we have a television and DVD player, the galley and the labs and sickbay. It's not the Hilton, but we're immeasurably more comfortable than the guys who came out here a century ago. I'm sorry about you having to share with Jake — I remember from our uni days how he used to snore all night!'

He laughed and Becky joined in.

'Anyway, we're a bit of a motley crew. There's a small film unit making a documentary, scientists, an artist. I'm what Jake calls the plankton guy, but it's a lot more serious than that. We don't know as much as we'd like about the smallest planktonic, Eukaryotes, and when you bear in mind that plankton are the foundation for the whole Antarctic marine ecosystem . . . ' he broke off and grinned. 'Sorry!'

'Hey, don't apologise,' she said, warming to him at once. 'It's very interesting. I'd like to know more.'

'Oh, you will,' he said. 'I'll bore you to death given half a chance.'

'I very much doubt that,' she said and suddenly noticed Jake had appeared behind Alex and he wasn't looking at all happy.

'What's going on?' he said his eyes ablaze with suspicion.

'Just introducing myself to our new doctor,' Alex said, frowning at Jake. 'Is there something wrong?'

Lapis eyes flashed from Becky to Alex and back again.

'Nothing's wrong,' he said, his tone as icy as the roaring wind outside.

'Anyway, see you at dinner, Becky,' Alex said. 'And don't forget to get Jake to give you the guided tour.'

Jake waited until Alex had gone and his footsteps had faded into the distance before turning on Becky.

'Don't even think about getting your hooks into Alex,' he said. 'He's a happily married man and I happen to be very fond of him and his wife — and he's got kids too.'

Becky's skin prickled with humiliation, but she was determined not to let him see how much he'd rattled her.

'And I bet you're their godfather, too, aren't you?'

'As a matter of fact I am,' he replied.

She raised her chin. 'Well, I have no intention of getting my hooks, as you put it, into anyone.'

'Good,' he said, but he wouldn't meet her gaze.

He knows he's wrong about me, Becky thought, but he wasn't going to forgive in a hurry. And if she was honest with herself, she didn't blame him.

'Alex said something about a guided tour,' she said, her tone conciliatory. 'If you've time right now, I'd love to see round the ship.'

Amazingly he smiled. 'That's why I came back. I remembered after I'd left the cabin that I was supposed to be showing you round. If you're ready?'

'As I'll ever be,' she said.

Apparently without thinking, he took her arm and when she looked at his hand he made no move to remove it.

'It's pretty rough out there,' he explained. 'Best if you hang on to me. I guess you know your geography about the region?' he added as they stepped out of the cabin.

'I know there's little daylight at the moment,' she said.

'None at all. It's not the best time of year to visit the Antarctic,' he said. 'But at least we won't have tourists to contend with yet and we'll be here to catch the beginning of summer before the tours begin. Something to do with his studies of the marine ecosystem — Alex could tell you more about that than I can.'

It was hard to imagine tourists getting in the way, but Becky had done her homework and knew that it was becoming an increasingly popular holiday destination among the more adventurous.

The ship pitched and Becky was glad to have Jake's arm to hang on to.

'There's a rule when you're on

board,' Jake said. 'Always keep one hand free for the rail. The Southern ocean is like nothing you have ever encountered before.'

'Is this the Antarctic Convergence?' she asked.

'I don't believe so,' Jake replied. 'Best ask Simon.'

They entered the mess where someone was sitting alone pouring over marine charts.

'Simon Doubleday, this is Becky Hope — sorry, Callaghan — our second doctor,' Jake said. 'Becky, this is Simon who is an oceanographer.'

Simon rose, offering his hand to Becky. He was tall, thin and obviously rather shy.

'Hi, Simon,' Becky said. 'I was just asking Jake about the Antarctic Convergence and he said you were the guy to talk to.'

'Oh, yes, sure,' he said. 'Sit down. I'll explain. Basically it's where two very different waters meet and mix. The difference in temperature, salinity and density is quite marked and the Convergence is a very important place for algae, krill and so on. Nutrients rise up from the ocean floor at the Convergence,' he raised his arms to demonstrate.

His enthusiasm drove away his shyness and Becky was dimly aware of Jake seating himself at another table, stretching his long lean legs in front of him. She glanced at him briefly and saw he was watching her.

She had to force herself to listen to what Simon was telling her, all the time aware of Jake's eyes boring into her.

'But it's far more important than that,' Simon went on. 'This dense, oxygen rich, cold sea water drops to the ocean floor and travels north, cooling temperate and tropical seas. The Convergence is vital to the climate of our whole planet.'

'Fascinating,' Becky said truthfully. 'And where is it?'

'It varies from year to year and indeed from season to season,' Simon explained. 'You can't see it. In fact you wouldn't know it was there except when the ship's instruments detect a marked change in temperature.'

Becky leaned on the table, looking at the map he had spread out before him. By the time another guy entered the mess, Simon was actually quite animated and talkative.

'David Pollard,' the new arrival said, introducing himself. 'I must say you're a damn sight better looking than our other doctor. Oh, hi there, Jake. Didn't see you sitting there.'

Jake made a gruff growling noise in his throat.

'I'm the producer and director with the film crew,' David went on.

'Really?' Becky's interest turned to him. 'And what are you hoping to film? Penguins? Seals?'

'Anything and everything we see,' David said, pulling out a chair and joining Becky and Simon at the table.

* * *

More men arrived in the mess and soon Jake couldn't see Becky for bodies gathered round the table. They'd pulled up extra chairs and some were even sitting on the tables surrounding hers. She'd been like that at the hospital, only he'd been too blind to see it. She'd been open, friendly and had a knack of putting people at their ease whether they were patients, families or members of staff.

He'd been stupid to think that her friendliness towards him had meant anything more than it did. It didn't explain that night, though — he doubted anything ever would — but at least he could see now where he'd gone wrong. Maybe he'd allowed himself to get infatuated to the point where he'd been blinded to the real Becky Hope. Callaghan. Why the name change?

It suddenly felt very stuffy in the mess and he rose to his feet and left the room unnoticed only to bump into Alex outside the door.

'Not leaving are you? It's almost supper time,' Alex said. 'And cook's made us a delicious hoosh.'

'You're joking,' Jake grimaced. 'Penguin stew?'

'Chicken casserole actually,' Alex laughed. 'Don't worry, we won't make you eat seal steaks and penguin wings. For one thing we're not allowed to eat the wildlife and for another, I've heard it's pretty fishy.'

Jake turned and went back into the mess.

'What's going on?' Alex said when he saw the huddle of bodies clustered around one table.

'Becky Callaghan,' Jake replied with a hint of acid in his voice. 'That's what's going on.'

'You do know her,' Alex murmured. 'I thought you did. I sensed something between you. Ye gods, Jake! Don't tell me this that she's what you came all this way to escape from?'

Jake managed to tell him all he wanted to know with just a simple look.

'Well, nothing we can do about it now,' Alex said.

Jake knew that well enough. It was an awkward and frustrating dinner.

When it was time to turn in, Jake told Becky to go ahead.

'I'll be at least an hour,' he told her and she was grateful.

There was no room in the cabin for leaving clothes lying around, so she got into her pyjamas, then tidied everything else away. And as she slid under the covers, she barely noticed the roll of the ship.

Sleep, blessed sleep, she thought and closed her eyes hoping against hope that Jake would stay out of her dreams.

Try as she might, she couldn't get the man out of her mind. Get Jake Lachlan out of her mind — that was a joke as things had turned out!

Mercifully she felt her mind drift as the ship rocked her to sleep.

And she woke some time later to a clatter and a whispered curse.

Her eyes flashed open. She was facing the wall and the only light in the cabin came from Jake's bunk overhead.

Her stomach coiled inside her as she realised Jake was now in the cabin with her. Preparing for bed and trying his hardest to be quiet about it.

He'd had a shower. She was aware of the clean, fresh smell of him.

She gasped but he didn't hear as he knocked something else over.

'Damn,' he hissed. Becky couldn't help smiling as she imagined him fumbling around, desperate not to wake her. He was being thoughtful. Kind. Or perhaps he was simply watching his own back. After all, wasn't he alone in a small cabin with a man-eater? He'd every right to be scared.

Becky remained quiet, keeping her breathing steady and biting hard on her lip to stop herself bursting into laughter. It wasn't just his noisy attempts at being quiet that made her want to laugh, but a combination of tiredness and a sense of the ridiculous at this impossible situation they had now found themselves in.

For someone who was so good with

his hands, so precise with his movements and so skilful with a needle, Jake was a pretty poor cabin mate.

There was a small jolt as his hands clasped the ladder to the upper bunk, then a moment's hesitation. He was watching her sleeping. She could feel the hair at the back of her neck prickling as she felt his eyes boring into her.

What was he thinking? That he'd like to hurl her overboard at the earliest opportunity? Feed her to the leopard seals or the killer whales?

She made a small involuntary sound and suddenly the ladder creaked slightly as Jake hauled himself up into the upper bunk. She heard him sigh as he got himself quietly comfortable. What was he thinking? Suddenly his voice, slightly muted, broke the silence.

'You asleep, Callaghan?'

She rolled onto her back and stared at the bottom of the bunk above.

'Callaghan?' she repeated.

'It's your name isn't it? Helps me to

remember to . . . If you'd rather, I . . . '

'Callaghan's fine,' she replied airily.

'Did I wake you?'

'No,' she lied.

'Good,' he said. 'Goodnight then. Get a good night in because when we reach the Weddell Sea things are likely to get really rough.'

'Worse than this?'

'You bet.'

'Goodnight, Jake,' she said, thinking it was going to be impossible to go back to sleep now with so many thoughts raging through her head. But sleep came back and took her with it and if she dreamt of anything at all, she didn't remember what.

★　★　★

Above her Jake lay awake long after he heard her breathing change when she fell asleep and now it was early morning already.

Callaghan. He liked it. He could hardly bear to think her name, let alone say it, but he had to call her something. Callaghan was easier to handle. Just a name change, but it was a start.

Jake hesitated, his hand poised above her shoulder which was poking out of the covers. How was he supposed to wake her without touching her? He'd been calling her name for ages and she'd slept on, peacefully, blissfully unaware that he was there.

'Becky,' he said one more time. 'Callaghan, wake up.'

Absolutely no response.

'Oh, hell,' he muttered and reached out, closing his fingers over her shoulder. How could a shoulder be so sexy? And one clad in soft blue pyjamas at that? He could feel her bones and muscles, the heat of her skin beneath the fabric. He couldn't help thinking she felt skinnier than she had when . . . when last he'd held her.

'Callaghan,' he almost shouted as he gave her shoulder a firm shake. 'Wake up, will you?'

She stirred and as she turned over he

moved his hand away quickly, stepping back as far as the confines of the cabin would allow, placing as much distance between them as possible.

Splashes of violet in the morning pale of her face regarded him with some surprise. But there were still dark shadows beneath her eyes and a deep sadness exposed by her waking unawareness.

'Did I oversleep?' she asked, concerned. Her hair was sticking out at all angles and there was a red mark on her cheek where she'd been sleeping with her hand under it.

She looked lovely.

'No,' he said briskly, turning away from her. 'It's still early. I thought you might not want to miss this. Bring your camera if you have one and wear your insulated clothing and your flotation gear.'

'We're going up on deck?' she blinked.

'Deck operations have commenced,' he replied hurrying towards the door.

'And Alex might send out a Zodiac later. He'll want a doctor along, but you'll have to fight me for it. I'll wait for you in the mess.'

He paused with his hand on the door.

'Oh, and there's coffee there if you want it,' he said, pointing to a mug sitting on the desk.

'Much appreciated,' she murmured huskily. 'Jake, what . . . ?'

'Don't be too long,' he said and with that, hurried out of the cabin, locking the door behind him.

5

Jake rose from his chair as soon as Becky entered the mess. 'Ready? You are going to just love this!' he said, forgetting himself in his enthusiasm.

'It just looks dark out there. Dark sea scattered with ice. That's all.'

'All?' he breathed in exasperation. 'Come with me, Callaghan, and prepare for the sight of your life.'

'The ship isn't moving,' she said. 'And the wind has dropped. Have we anchored already?'

'These conditions will only be temporary,' he said with a rueful smile. 'These are the most violent, treacherous seas in the world. That's why I want you to see this before it changes.'

Becky followed him out onto the deck where ice clung to the rails — and she stopped dead in her tracks, her breath lodged in her throat. He was right. This was the sight of her life.

'Well?' he murmured. 'Glad I woke you?'

'Oh, Jake,' she said, instinctively looping her arm through his, wanting somehow to thank him for thinking of her, for waking her up so she could witness this amazing sight. 'It's fantastic.'

It would be a few weeks until the Antarctic sunrise, but before her lay the Weddell Sea bathed in silver moonlight. The sky was almost black, spangled with a million stars and beneath it the ice pack was shimmering white against the black of the sea.

Not flat as she would have expected it to be, but instead covered in hummocks and lumps.

'Shackleton kept his men alive on that ice for months,' Jake murmured. 'Imagine. Somewhere under that ice, deep in that sea lie the remains of the Endurance. And they crossed from the ice pack to Elephant Island in three small boats, twenty-eight exhausted men. I don't know how they survived.'

'Determination,' Becky said. Despite all her warm gear, she was beginning to feel cold.

'Hey,' Jake whispered suddenly and put his arm around her, bending down so that his face was beside hers. 'Look.'

She was conscious only of his warm cheek against hers and suddenly she didn't feel cold at all. In fact, she felt as if she could stand all day on the deck, close to him, looking out over this amazing, unique seascape.

'What am I looking for?' she asked as his beard tickled her face.

She laughed nervously and he seemed to realise they were standing far too close and drew away, removing his arm and pointing instead into the distance. He'd got caught up in the moment, that was all. Just as she had. And he seemed just as disturbed by their unthinking contact.

'Weddell Seals,' Jake said, his voice hoarse.

He wasn't looking at the seals. He

was looking at her. She wasn't looking at the seals either. Her mouth felt as dry as a bone. She moistened her lips behind the cover of her scarf. Thank goodness she was wearing sunglasses or he might have seen the naked truth in her eyes.

'Those aren't Weddell Seals, Jake,' Alex's voice interrupted. He came to stand between them and handed Jake a pair of binoculars. 'Crabeaters,' he corrected. 'Smaller and more stream-lined than Weddells.'

Jake looked, then handed the binoculars to Becky. 'Quite a sizeable group for Crabeaters,' he said.

'Do they eat crabs?'

'You tell her,' Alex said.

'They eat Antarctic krill,' Jake said. 'They have oddly shaped teeth which interlock and form a kind of sieve for that purpose. They have beautiful dog-like faces. I'm actually rather fond of them.'

'Even if they do have a tendency to bare their teeth and snort foul breath at you,' Alex laughed.

'Well, it's thought they might be monogamous,' Jake said quietly. 'That's always a plus point in my book.'

Ouch, Becky thought.

'We'll launch a Zodiac,' Alex went on briskly. 'It's difficult to observe them on the ice at this time of year, but while the weather is with us at the moment we can't miss the opportunity.'

'I'd like to come, Alex,' Becky said.

Alex looked at Jake. 'That all right with you?'

'No,' Jake said tightly. 'It isn't. I told you you'd have to fight me for this, Callaghan, and I meant every word.'

'Hey, come on children, lighten up. There'll be plenty of opportunities for both of you. What's your problem with Becky coming along too, Jake?'

'I don't think she's ready to go out on the ice. She only got down here yesterday. It's too soon.'

Alex ran his fingers through his beard. 'Jake has a point, Becky,' he said. 'I'm sorry, but this time its Jake's party.'

Decisions were made fast down here, Becky realised as she enviously watched the men head towards the pack. Weather conditions could change so quickly, even an ice breaker like the Delphinus could be crushed in the ice. For the first time she appreciated the dangerous nature of their mission. However they were in constant contact with their nearest land base and the real possibility of rescue if the worst were to happen. She wasn't afraid and was quite startled to realise that if she had had any misgivings, knowing that Jake was along made her feel more secure. Secure physically perhaps. She wasn't so sure about emotionally.

She closed her eyes and breathed in. The smell of this place was like nothing she'd ever experienced before, the smell of absolute, pure coldness. It was a whole new experience for her senses. The endless stillness except for the occasional cracking of the ice was so complete.

At that moment Becky thought she

would never tire of looking across the ice. And the Zodiac was so far away now, she couldn't distinguish one man from another. Any of those dark shadowy figures moving onto the pack could be Jake.

And what if the ice fractured? Or a whale upended the floe they were on? Were there whales this far south in winter? Jake could be tipped into that icy water. Suddenly she didn't want to watch any more and turned away.

The crew on the Zodiac would be gone all day. This could well turn out to be bearable. But on the other hand, if he was going to act like a spoilt kid every time an opportunity to go on the ice came up, it wasn't going to be much of a trip for her.

* * *

Jake looked up and saw the reassuring lights of the Delphinus in the distance. The pack wasn't as stable as Alex had first thought. There had been a couple of hairy moments when fissures had appeared in the ice and huge chunks had broken free.

There was only a mild swell beneath the large floe they'd finally settled on and Jake hunkered down to get a close up shot of a Crabeater seal who didn't seem all that pleased to be photographed.

He could see Adelie Penguins too, a whole hoard of them milling about on the ice some distance away.

He glanced back at the ship again and wondered if Becky was among those figures still on deck. Wondered if she was still glowering after him, furious that he'd stolen her chance to walk on the ice.

But how could he let the wretched girl wander around out here? It was a dangerous place. She was skin and bone and an accidental dunking in that icy sea would probably kill her in seconds. And what if she decided flirting with the guys was more important than safety? He hated himself for that thought. She wasn't stupid. She wasn't his responsibility either.

Around midday when a faint light temporarily dispelled the darkness, they stopped to eat the rations they'd brought with them.

'How many weeks is it until sun up?' Jake asked, nodding towards the eerie twilight.

'Three,' Simon said absently. 'I would have thought Becky would have wanted to come today.'

Jake felt an inexplicable twinge of jealousy. It was too much to expect the other guys not to be aware of her feminine presence.

'I said . . . '

'I heard what you said,' Jake replied somewhat sharply. 'She'll have other opportunities. You're not married are you, Simon?'

'Well, no, I . . . I don't really . . . um . . . '

He sensed Simon backing off a little and watched as he nervously fiddled with his glasses under his visor. What was he doing? He hadn't meant to upset the guy. He seemed a sensitive, rather shy person and the last thing Jake wanted was to crush anyone.

'Have you gathered much material?' he asked, rather more kindly.

'Er, yes,' Simon said holding up his case of various instruments and relaxing now that he was on firmer ground. 'I only mentioned Becky because she seemed so interested in what we'd be doing down here. You appear to know quite a lot, but . . . '

'No need to explain,' Jake said, his manner conciliatory. 'I didn't mean anything, I assure you.'

He clapped his hand on Simon's shoulder and gave it a squeeze through the thick layers of clothing.

'Jake,' a call went up from the film crew. 'Can you give us a hand over here, please, mate?'

'Duty calls,' Jake grinned.

'Sure,' Simon said. 'If anyone asks, I'm just going to slip over there and see if I can drag up some more samples.'

Jake turned and tramped across to where the film crew were filming the antics of a seal that seemed determined to put on a show for them.

'You'll need to be my sound man,' David Pollard said. 'My guy over there is feeling a bit queasy.'

'I'll take a look at him,' Jake said, starting towards a guy who was sitting down on the ice a few feet away.

'He's fine,' David said. 'I didn't call you over to look at him. I don't want to lose this opportunity.'

He clamped a pair of headphones over Jake's head and handed him a boom mike, then told him exactly what was required of him. Jake was concerned about the guy sitting on the ice, but could understand him feeling a bit odd.

It was disorientating to be on the ice and took some getting used to.

That's something to add to my CV, he thought with a grin as he operated the mike. Sound man.

They filmed the seal for half an hour

before he tired of showing off his antics to the men and moved away to join the rest of his family group.

'We're going to pack up now and head back to the ship,' Alex said and Jake knew that behind all those clothes, Alex was laughing at him.

'Is that great furry thing in your hand a boom mike, or . . . ?' Alex laughed.

'Mind your own business,' Jake laughed right back at him. 'I'm making myself useful, just like you told me to.'

'Back to the Zodiac everyone,' Alex turned and called out. 'Weather's deteriorating. Let's move, people.'

They gathered up equipment and samples and hurried across the ice. The wind was picking up quite rapidly now. Jake could feel the icy sting on its breath even through his clothing.

As they loaded the Zodiac, Alex turned to Jake.

'Have you seen Simon?' he asked.

'Yeah, he was . . . ' Jake began and as he turned to show Alex where he'd last seen him, there was nothing but ice.

'He said he was going over there to gather more samples.'

'Anyone seen Simon?' Alex yelled. Nothing but the blank looks of several pairs of sunglasses met his enquiry.

An icy chill had gripped Jake's stomach, far colder than anything the Antarctic winter could produce. He grabbed his medical bag and he and Alex ran as fast as terrain and heavy clothing allowed towards the place where Simon had been last seen.

Alex swore loudly as he ran and tripped over a ridge of ice. Jake kept on running and clambering over hummocks. They were supposed to look out for each other out here, but with so much to do and so much going on, Simon had been lost.

★ ★ ★

Jake saw him first, a sodden patch of darkness in the moonlit white of the ice. Just his head and shoulders visible.

'Here!' Jake bellowed. 'Bring ropes!'

Simon's box stood on the ice, but the equipment he'd been using to take the samples had vanished into a narrow fissure. He must have tried to retrieve the equipment and slipped into the water.

By some miracle, the fissure he'd slipped through wasn't open all the way down and he was standing on a ledge of ice beneath the water. He was too far down to haul himself and the weighty sodden clothing he wore out, but high enough so that his head and shoulders were above the water.

'Jake,' he gasped. 'Can't . . . '

'Hold on, Simon,' Jake called. 'We'll get you out of there.'

Jake dropped his bag and fell to his knees in one swift movement, reaching out trying to haul Simon out of the hole.

'What the hell are you doing?' Alex yelled. 'Hold back, that's an order. Wait for ropes so we can do this properly.'

'No time,' Jake said urgently. 'Help me here. Grab his arm, Alex! If we

78

don't get him out of there now, he's a dead man.'

There was an ominous groan from the ice and the fissure began to heal as the pack began to close in on itself.

★   ★   ★

The men in the Zodiac wore identical red jackets, but one of them had been stripped of his clothes and wrapped in blankets. Becky gripped the rail, feeling the burn of ice through her thick mittens. There'd been a message from Alex — they were bringing in a casualty, hypothermic, get the sickbay ready, warm some IV fluid.

'Who is it?' Luke asked.

Luke was a trained first aider and was standing by to assist Becky if it should be required.

The guys on the Zodiac were taking it easy. A sudden jolt could cause cardiac arrest. Hypothermic patients had to be handled with utmost care. Jake would know that, she thought. The casualty couldn't be him.

It was a pointless thought. Everyone on these trips knew how to handle a hypothermic patient. Which left her with the thought that it could be him; that huddled, blanketed figure could be Jake. And the thought that he could be hurt stirred like a venomous snake inside her.

The brief midday twilight had faded and whatever light there had been from the moon had vanished leaving a complete darkness and a wind rapidly gathering intensity.

'Steady,' Jake's voice, firm and commanding rang out as they moved the casualty onto the ship and Becky's legs went weak with relief. 'You ready for us up there, Callaghan?'

'Ready and waiting,' she called back.

It was serious whoever it was and she was wrong to be any more concerned about Jake than anyone else. He was just one of the guys wasn't he? Who are you kidding, Callaghan? Jake's more than just one of the guys.

'It's Simon,' Alex said grimly. 'God knows how long he was in the water. He's barely conscious.'

'We got him out in time,' Jake said calmly. 'He'll be all right.'

'Yeah?' Alex turned on him. 'Well he shouldn't have gone off on his own out there. That fissure could have opened up and he wouldn't even have seen it until it was too late.'

Jake turned on Alex. These guys were supposed to be best friends, so what was going on? They were measuring up to each other like a pair of warring stags. The other guys looked on, keeping a wary distance as if they knew better than to interfere.

'And just what the hell were you thinking?' Alex roared, his face right in Jake's. 'What the hell were you playing at? You could have . . . Jesus, Jake! Why do you always have to take that one extra step over the damn line?'

Jake stood still, unflinching, bearing the brunt of Alex's anger, but he said nothing, then he turned to Becky.

'What are you standing around here for? Let's get this guy to the sickbay. Have you got everything ready?'

She nodded, then glanced at Alex who was no longer glowering and furious, but looked almost devastated.

'Everyone else,' Alex said quietly. 'Get into dry, warm clothes.'

Speedily, but with utmost care, Becky and Luke transferred Simon to the sickbay, and it was only as they arrived there that she realised Jake who was following along behind, was leaving a wet trail behind him.

'You're wet,' she said.

'Yeah, and you're not so bright yourself! Well spotted, Callaghan.'

She could do without his dry sarcasm. It didn't become him.

'Is Alex wet too?'

'No.'

'Get out of those clothes, Jake,' she said.

'Well, Callaghan,' Jake said. 'I had no idea you felt that way about me. Do I have time for a bath first?'

'What?' she snapped, confused by this strange, unprofessional Jake. What was wrong with the man? Had that chip on his shoulder addled his brain? 'Get serious, Jake.'

She helped Simon onto the bed and slipped a Heibler jacket onto him to warm his trunk, then placed an oxygen mask over his face.

'All right, Simon. I'm going to start warming you up . . .'

'Slowly,' Jake called from the corner where he was struggling to peel off his wet clothes.

'Slowly, as Jake says,' she continued, pressing back her irritation. 'You know the drill, Simon. I have to get your core temperature up which means just heating your trunk. I know you're uncomfortable, but if I heat your extremities at this stage, the cold blood will rush to your organs and your condition could worsen. You understand?'

He looked at her as if he didn't care. She glanced over her shoulder at Jake, then quickly returned her gaze to Simon. Jake was naked, shaking out a set of blue scrubs. She had no wish to see him like that.

Feeling her face heat up, she returned her full attention to Simon.

'I'm going to set up an IV drip now, Simon.'

She smiled reassuringly at him then at Luke who had the warmed IV fluid ready. She hung it on the stand, inserted the plastic spike into the connector port to perforate the seal, then gently squeezed the bag.

'Little scratch now, Simon.'

She set about introducing the intravenous cannula, watching for the flashback of blood before penetrating into the vein, then she removed the needle and advanced the cannula further along the vein.

'Want me to set up the ECG?' a voice said in her ear.

She turned to see Jake looming up behind her, looking over her shoulder, then checking the IV bag.

'I don't want you to do anything, Jake,' she said, aware of his body brushing against hers as he leaned over her. The scrubs were pretty thin and she could feel the icy coldness of his body against hers. 'Get warmed up. Have something warm and sweet to drink.'

Whoo, Jake thought as he reeled away from the bed where Simon was looking far more comfortable and somewhat warmer than when he'd hauled him out of the water.

It was amazing the speed that Becky moved about the sickbay. Checking Simon's pulse and respiration, adjusting the IV, dishing out orders to Luke. And he watched Luke watching Becky with that look of admiration in his eye.

Admiration for the way she carried out her job — or something else?

'She's too old for you,' he murmured under his breath, then realised Callaghan was staring at him.

'What did you say?' she demanded.

He felt strange. As if he were in one

of those movies where one person moves slowly while the rest of the world speeds past him. His whole body seemed to be moving at a different rate to everyone else.

Alex came in and Becky had to turn away from Jake so she could speak to him. Their voices sounded strange, disjointed as if they were speaking under water, then they started looking over at him. Talking. Looking. What were they saying?

Alex turned and walked across to him. His face seemed enormous with that great bushy black beard. It made Jake want to laugh.

'What's wrong, Jake?' he said. 'You feeling okay?'

Jake shook his head to try and clear it. A part of him knew what was happening, but he felt powerless to do anything about it.

And now Becky was marching over to him, her determined little face set, her too skinny body lost somewhere under too many clothes. Good thing she hadn't been on the ice today. She wouldn't have lasted two seconds in that water. She hadn't an ounce of fat on her to keep her warm.

'Not like me,' Jake said, grinning. He knew he was grinning and knew it was inappropriate, but wasn't quite sure why.

But he was sure of one thing. No way was he going to show any sign of weakness in front of Becky. He'd sort this out. Yes, that's what he'd do. No help required, thank you very much.

'His skin is still soaking wet,' Becky said. 'He's put the dry scrubs on without drying himself.'

Talking about me as if I'm not here?

He felt himself sinking as Alex helped him onto the other bed in the sickbay. Then something tickled his ear.

'Sit still, Jake,' Becky scolded. 'I'm trying to take your temperature. I can do it this way, or . . . '

Bossy. He'd seen it before. At the hospital when they worked together, he'd thought her a bossy little thing.

Kind, capable but bossy as hell.

And now she was fiddling with his legs, raising up his feet. What on earth did she think she was doing? She was supposed to be looking after the sick guy, not running round making him comfortable.

'You're not going to take advantage of me?' he asked as she leaned over him. He licked his lips, wondering if her lips still tasted the same. Sweet like wine and plump like juicy strawberries. 'I've no clothes on.'

'Thirty-five,' she said. Thirty-five what? Thirty-five kisses?

'No way, lady,' he said with a low chuckle, because whatever else might be happening, he was going to keep a grip on his heart. 'You aren't getting your hands on me no matter how much you want to.'

'Irrational and confused,' she said, but he could tell from the tone of her voice that she was embarrassed.

'Are you?' he said. 'Well, I'll put it into plain English for you shall I?'

'He doesn't know what he's saying,' Becky said.

'Hey, Jake,' Alex was beside him. 'Shut up! You're hypothermic. Just let Becky do her job and take care of you, huh?'

'She's good at that,' Jake said, then he could speak no more for she had placed an oxygen mask over his face.

6

Much later when he was feeling far closer to normal than he had previously been, Jake asked, 'Did I say anything inappropriate?' Do anything embarrassing?'

Becky looked at him and smiled. She leaned over him again to plump up his pillows. The worst of it was she'd enjoyed him flirting with her when he didn't know what he was saying. How wrong was that?

'Apart from dancing naked round the sickbay you mean?' she said, a glimmer of mischief in her violet eyes until she saw the uncertainty in Jake's eyes and retracted. 'You were as good as gold,' she lied through her teeth. 'Except you were hypothermic and you failed to tell anyone. It could have been serious. What if I'd sent you to your cabin and you'd collapsed? By the time you were found, it could have been too late.'

She knew it was unfair to put the blame squarely on his shoulders. He wasn't alone out there. Alex should have noticed.

'How's Simon?' he asked, changing the subject.

'Warming up,' she replied, glancing over her shoulder at Simon who was doing pretty well considering. 'I'm really pleased with him.'

'Alex?'

'Angry with you for some reason. What did you do, Jake?'

Jake's eyes scorched into her. 'I did what I was paid to do,' he said. Then he threw back the blanket and swung his legs off the bed.

His blazing eyes flung out a challenge.

'Look the other way, Callaghan,' he growled. 'Allow me some dignity.'

'Stay right where you are, Doctor,' Becky said, placing herself between him and his escape route. 'I'll say when you can get up. And as for averting my eyes

— I'm a doctor, you've nothing that I haven't seen before.'

He moved towards her and for a moment their bodies touched again. Becky held her position. He was going nowhere.

'I'm warm,' he said, grasping her hand against his chest. 'See?'

His skin certainly felt warm and although she struggled to keep her palm flat, her fingers curled against his skin, the tips of them moving across his chest almost as if they had a mind of their own. She could hardly breathe. To be this close . . .

She drew in her breath sharply, achingly and dropped her hand away.

'I feel fine,' he said gruffly and seemed about to move her aside, then thought better of it. Instead he stood perfectly still, looking down at her. Absently he reached out and touched the ends of her hair, staring at it as if his life depended upon it.

Becky felt as if she'd never breathe again. He was supposed to be well past the irrational phase now and making a direct course for normality. Yet nothing about this felt normal.

He dropped his hand away, but continued to look down at her.

'I don't have to spell it out to you, Jake,' she said, her voice calm despite the turmoil inside. 'You know you have to stay in that bed for at least 48 hours.'

'Damn,' he muttered and reluctantly got back into the bed. 'I know I wasn't that hypothermic.'

'You were,' she said as she gently pulled the cover back over him. 'I'm going to get some breakfast now and . . .'

'Breakfast?' He sat bolt upright. 'What do you mean, breakfast? I haven't been here all night?'

Indeed he had. Becky had sat in here all night with the two men, monitoring them at regular intervals, watching them sleep, particularly watching Jake, the rise and fall of his chest, the darkness of his lashes against his cheek.

But no, she only seemed to watch

him more because he had proved himself a master of deception, hiding his symptoms from her. She bit her lip. Look who's talking, she thought. When it came to matters of deception, then surely the award went to her.

'Anyway,' she said. 'Rod is going to sit in with you guys for a while. And Luke's preparing a special breakfast for you. I'll see you later. And if I hear you've been out of bed again, there'll be trouble. Understand?'

'Yes, sir,' Jake said and he gave her such a rueful smile that it was like a knife twisting in her gut.

She moved across the sickbay, spoke to Rod who was one of the film crew and who was one of those with first aid experience, then left without a backward glance.

* * *

'How are the patients?' Alex asked as he placed his tray down on the table opposite Becky. 'More to the point, how

94

are you? Tired? You'll get some rest today? You look all in, Becky.'

'I plan to,' she said. 'Simon and Jake are doing fine. There's still a possibility of complications, but I'm monitoring for that.'

'Yeah, well,' Alex said as he scooped up a fork piled high with scrambled egg. 'I meant what I said about you resting up. I know what you doctors can be like when it comes to your own health. Stubborn lot.'

'I don't know what you mean I'm sure,' Becky said.

'Sure you do. Thanks to Jake I nearly lost two men out there yesterday.'

'Simmer down, Alex,' she said, looking up at him. 'Or I'll be booking you into the sickbay with high blood pressure.'

'Simmer down?' he repeated. 'You'll be lucky if I start to simmer down this side of sunrise. Have you any idea how it felt to watch my chief medic — and my best friend, I might add — leap into that icy water? He wouldn't wait for ropes — oh, no, not Jake.'

Becky's appetite deserted her. Heroics like that were the actions of a man who didn't give a damn about his own life. Was that her doing too? Her throat felt tight and dry.

'I realised he'd got wet somehow,' she said lamely.

'Wet? The damn fool went right under. We were trying to pull Simon out — at Jake's insistence — when the ice ledge he was on collapsed and he sank beneath the water. Jake just went right on in behind him, hanging on to him. I thought I'd lost the pair of them.'

'But you didn't.'

He glared at her. 'No. But the pack was moving — it could have shut the door on them and they'd have been lost underneath it in a split second.'

Becky considered for a moment. She knew how Alex must have felt. She felt bad enough just hearing about it, but she knew how Jake would have felt too. He could never just stand by and watch another man drown.

'And if you'd waited for ropes?'

'That's beside the point,' Alex said, his rage deserting him. 'It's beside the damn point. I love that stupid guy. He's my kids' godfather for goodness sake. They adore him. What was I supposed to tell them? Hey kids, sorry but Uncle Jake jumped in and the ice slammed shut over his head?'

He pulled himself together and stared across the table at Becky. She was trying very hard not to imagine Jake trapped beneath the ice. It would have meant certain death. He could even have been crushed between two floes.

'And yet, if Jake hadn't jumped in first, you would have. Am I right?'

'You finished?' he asked.

'Yes, I . . . '

'Then get to your cabin and grab some sleep,' he said with a weary smile. 'That's an order.'

Becky rose. Her legs felt wobbly again. She was tired. She'd been tired yesterday when Jake woke her for that extra early start, but now it came crashing in on her.

Alex reached out and caught her hand in his.

'I know something happened between you and Jake,' he said. 'I don't know what because he hasn't told me. I do know that he was badly let down once. That's putting it mildly . . . You do know? What Thalia did to him . . . '

Her heart suddenly began to thud in her chest. No she didn't know.

'Thalia?'

'His ex-wife,' Alex said. 'He's just about over her, then suddenly he's keen to come down here with me. Why was that, Becky? Was it you?'

'If anyone needs me . . . ' she began and pulled her hand from his, letting him know she wasn't going to answer any questions about her personal connection with Jake.

'Jake and Simon are not to leave the sickbay,' she added.

'Oh, trust me,' Alex said. 'Those guys aren't going anywhere.'

She hesitated beside his chair.

'Just as a matter of interest, Alex,' she said. 'What would you have done if Jake hadn't gone in the water after Simon?'

He looked up at her through weary eyes and smiled. 'I've got two kids waiting for me at home,' he said. 'If I'd stood by and watched a guy drown, I would never have been able to look them in the eye again.'

'Then don't be so hard on Jake,' she said. 'He doesn't need it.'

She didn't want to elaborate, so turned quickly and headed back to her cabin to catch up on some sleep.

★　★　★

'Stop fussing,' Jake said. 'It's over, okay? Just just leave me alone.'

'I'm sorry,' Becky said, backing away. 'I was only . . . '

It was his first night back sleeping in the cabin and she had to admit, if only to herself, that he looked absolutely fine. The only difference seemed to be that he was even more determined to hold her at arm's length.

And he'd been hurt before. Had Thalia cheated on him?

'Well whatever it is you were only trying to do, don't,' he said. 'I don't need it, Becky. I'd prefer you to keep your distance if you don't mind.'

She looked around their cramped cabin, then at him and spread her arms helplessly.

'Maybe I should get Alex to build us an extension,' she said and to her pleased amazement, Jake burst out laughing.

'This is kind of ridiculous isn't it,' he said, relaxing visibly. 'The two of us, stuck here together. When I think how long I spent trying to get a date with you and how it all ended up and now here we are, sharing the same cabin, the same breathing space.'

'It's a tough call, but someone has to do it,' Becky said, trying to keep it light, trying to make him laugh again. 'You seem to think I'm after your body, Jake.

All I was offering to do was pass you your dressing gown.'

'Can you blame me?' he asked. 'You wanted me once.'

Her face burned with anger and shame. He just wasn't going to make any of this easy for her. Not at all. She'd tried to keep it light, tried to be friends with him, but every time she got anywhere close, he had to refer back to that night as if their whole relationship and all the time they'd known each other before that counted for nothing.

Didn't he think it hurt her to think about it too? Had he honestly never given a thought to how she might feel in all this? Right now, she was just too tired to care.

'Have it your way,' she said. 'You just carry on punishing me, because ultimately it's yourself you're damaging, Jake.'

'Oh?' he said. 'And how do you figure that out, Callaghan?'

'Because you've changed already,' she said, her voice heavy with sadness and regret. 'And I'm ashamed of the part I had to play in that change. I'm not proud of what I did to you, Jake, to either of us. But it makes me even sadder to see what it's done to you. You were a nice man.'

He regarded her for a long while, his lapis eyes glittering like crystals of ice on midnight water.

'Don't be sad for me, Callaghan,' he said, his voice as brittle as the ice on the deck rails outside. 'You should be happy. You opened my eyes once and for all and you've guaranteed I will never, ever, be made a fool of again.'

She shrank back from him. 'I never took you for a fool,' she said.

'Maybe not, but you made me into one,' he said. 'And I won't forget that. And what about your husband? Where does he fit into all this? How come you can just take off and leave him?'

It was the first time he'd mentioned Bryn and she was unprepared for the shock of it. It had been all too easy to almost forget he ever existed and her former life with Bryn had taken on the quality of a bad dream.

'No answers for me, huh?' he went on, his lip curling in a way that made her want to hate him. 'I thought as much. That kind of arrangement might suit some people, but it sure doesn't suit me.'

'It's not like that, Jake,' she said softly.

This was her chance to tell him that Bryn was dead, but somehow the words wouldn't come out because she feared his reaction.

'Isn't it? Then what is it like, Becky? You tell me.'

The sudden use of her name was like a fist closing around her throat. And far from wanting to put distance between them, he came closer so that it was she who was backing away until she felt her back touch the wall.

What happened next took them both by surprise. Jake reached out suddenly and cupped his hand round the back of her neck, his touch sending bolts of electricity down her spine. He pulled her towards him, hesitating only for a fraction of a second before kissing her.

Becky couldn't escape if she wanted to, not unless she could find a way of melting into the wall behind her. But she didn't want to melt anywhere except in Jake's arms.

His hand still cupped the back of her neck, his fingers moving slowly in her hair, every second that passed a painful reminder of what she was missing, what she'd thrown away. A reminder of how she ached for him.

He'd had to do something about that look on her face. She had looking hurt and confused down to a fine art and the only way to block it out, stop it getting to him, was to block it from view and he did that by kissing her.

What he didn't fully expect was her response. And like that night she came to his apartment, her lips trembled beneath his, as if she was fighting tears. But why? Did he even care? Not at this moment. His brain had gone into meltdown. He loved her . . .

The clanging of the alarm brought him to his senses and he pushed her roughly away. Thank God for Alex and his drills! Love? This wasn't love. This was something else. Something tawdry. He wiped the back of his hand across his mouth as if he'd just eaten something disagreeable.

'Very clever, Callaghan,' he grated. 'Almost had me there for a moment, didn't you?'

'No, Jake, I . . . it was you . . . '

Bewildered, she got up and fumbled for her jacket and tried to pull it on. The sleeves were inside out. How could he be so cruel? To kiss her like that and then blame her? She was shaking like a leaf as his rejection set in.

Rejection — huh! She should be used to that kind of pain by now!

She hadn't instigated that. He was the one who'd started it. But it didn't really matter who started it. What mattered was that they both clearly still wanted each other as much, if not more than ever. At least it was true for her. She loved the guy. Didn't matter how mean he was, how much he pushed her away and made her feel dirty and unworthy, she still loved him.

She floundered and fumbled and cursed under her breath and tried to keep the tears of humiliation and shame at bay as the heat of the insulated jacket and the scorch of humiliation choked her.

Then suddenly the jacket was removed, Jake quickly pulled the sleeves the right way out, then handed it back to her, his eyes colder than she had ever seen them before.

'See you on deck, Callaghan,' he said. 'I'll tell Alex you're on your way.'

But when he'd gone and the door had shut behind him, she collapsed to the floor, her arms enfolding her legs as she rested her head on her knees, bitter tears coursing down her face.

If it was revenge he'd been after, then he'd done it well. Even when Bryn had left her, he hadn't left her feeling this broken, this shattered and empty.

7

Some of the other guys were shivering. They'd come up on deck in their dressing gowns, drilled to answer the alarms at once. She shouldn't have taken the time to put on her jacket, but she needed the time to compose herself. She'd spent the last five minutes at the sink, splashing cold water on her face and holding a wet flannel against her swollen eyes.

'You all right, Becky? What kept you?' Alex asked tersely.

She felt small and slumped inside her thick outdoor gear. She felt a very long way from all right. She'd pulled her scarf round her face. Jake's beard had left tiny red marks on her skin and she didn't want anyone to know what had happened — or almost happened — back in her cabin. She didn't want them to see her red eyes and they were all looking at her. She wanted to run, but where could she run to? So she had no choice but to stand, bearing their scrutiny, enduring their curiosity and facing up to Alex's anger.

'I thought I'd made it clear how important it is to attend these drills as soon as you hear the alarm,' Alex said coldly. 'If this had been a genuine real emergency . . .'

'Leave it, Alex,' Jake interrupted, reaching out and holding his friend's arm. 'We all knew it was a drill and I told you Becky was on her way.'

'Makes no difference, Jake,' Alex said. 'It's why we have the drills, so we know everyone can make it to their lifeboat stations without delay.'

'Get off her back, Alex,' Jake murmured softly, unwittingly echoing Becky's own words to Alex about Jake. 'She doesn't need it.'

Could he see? Could he see how much she was hurting? How could she ever know when he wouldn't let her get close?

'Alex is right,' Becky said, her voice a

croaky rustle under her scarf. 'I'm sorry I was tardy. It won't happen again. I apologise everyone if I messed up the drill and kept you all waiting.'

'Apology accepted,' Alex said, but his eyes were still on Jake.

★ ★ ★

'You're worried about what people might think?' Jake said incredulously as Becky watched him packing up his things when they were back in their cabin half an hour after the drill. 'Are you serious?'

She bit her lip. Maybe him moving into the sickbay and using one of the hospital beds as his own was a good idea, but what if they had an emergency and needed the beds?

'If I stay in here with you, I won't be answerable for what happens,' he said, his voice as rough as sandpaper. 'You know it and I know it. You don't seem to have any kind of self control at all and I . . . '

'You do?' she laughed hollowly, her laughter echoing the emptiness inside. 'Come on, Jake, this isn't entirely my fault.'

'No, no, you're right,' he said, raking his hand through his hair, then rasping his fingers in his beard. 'God, I hate this thing. It makes me feel like some kind of caveman.'

He looked at her then, really looked at her, his lapis eyes blinking as he took in the chafing on her face. Reaching out with fingers that sent rivers of fire rushing across her skin, he touched the red patches.

'Was this me?'

'Your beard,' she said, turning away from his hand.

'I'm sorry,' he said. 'I have something you can put on to soothe that.'

'I've already put something on it,' she said. 'It'll be gone by morning. Don't worry, no one need know what it is.'

'I wasn't worried,' he said lightly. 'And if anyone asks why I'm sleeping in the sickbay, I'll tell them it's because your snoring keeps me awake.'

She held the door open for him.

Jake nodded and brushed past her as he left, not giving her a second glance as he strode off down the corridor towards the sickbay.

She shut the door firmly. She turned and peered in the mirror. She wished she'd brought some make up along if only to cover those red marks. But she could pass them off as windburn which was exactly what she did at breakfast the next morning.

'Will you be all right to come out on the ice?' Alex asked.

She looked around the mess where all the men were tucking in to scrambled eggs, bacon and beans.

'Don't look for Jake's approval,' Alex said. 'He's not shown up for breakfast yet anyway. I'm asking you. We've got a window of decent weather and I want to make use of it. Are you up for it?'

'Yes,' she said.

He stood beside her table for a moment, then pulled out a chair and sat down. She poked her fork into her eggs and twirled it clockwise. She had absolutely no appetite at all, but knew if she was to go out on to the freezing ice pack then she must eat.

'Becky, if you've got any problems, it's important we sort them out. Living in each other's pockets like this, there's no room for disputes and any niggles need to be ironed out before they become major bones of contention,' Alex said.

'I don't have any problems,' she said, levelling her eyes at his.

'Be on deck at ten, then,' he said briskly. 'And wrap up warm.'

Becky was just leaving her cabin when Jake came charging down the corridor. She couldn't believe her eyes. His beard had gone. Seeing him clean shaven gave her a jolt, reminded her of just how good looking he was.

Not only had the beard gone, so had the mane of golden hair. He'd had it cut almost viciously short, but it made him look even more masculine than the beard had. She realised that a lot of the blondeness had been caused by the sun. Short, his hair was much darker. It made him look very different, almost dangerous. And his eyes were even more startlingly blue.

'You're not going on the ice,' he said flatly. 'I'll go in your place.'

'I didn't come all this way to sit on my backside in the warm and not see anything,' Becky said indignantly. 'And besides, it's up to Alex who he takes on the ice, not you.'

He towered over her, but his shoulders slumped.

'Don't do this, Becky,' he said wearily. 'If you're going out there to punish me . . . '

'In what way would me stepping onto the ice be punishing you?' she asked, cocking her head on one side.

'If anything happens to you . . . '

Those five words hit her like an axe between the eyes.

They implied that he really cared.

'Oh, Jake,' she murmured, then came

to her senses. It was no use kidding herself that he cared. Why should he? She tilted her chin. 'I'm not stupid,' she said.

'No one ever said you were. It looks beautiful out there on the ice, especially on a day like this with the sky clear and the moon shining down, but don't be fooled. It's treacherous out there, probably the most dangerous place on earth.'

Right here, right now felt more like the most dangerous place on earth to Becky. The ice would be easy after this. 'Excuse me, Jake,' she said calmly, quietly. 'I don't want to keep Alex waiting and have him mad at me again.'

He looked down at her for a long, long moment, then sighed heavily and stepped to one side.

'Thank you,' she whispered and walked past him.

'Callaghan . . . Becky,' he called to her retreating back. 'Take care.'

Her shoulders stiffened and she nodded, but she didn't look back.

This was wonderful. Becky had never been surrounded by such complete and utter silence as she was at this moment, not even in the Arctic had she felt this far away from everything.

It was like finding yourself on a different planet, part of a whole new universe where the stars shone brighter than in any other place and the ice twinkled and shone in the day that was still night.

The men worked around her, some filming, some gathering samples. One man was busy gathering the animal waste left on the ice that would, Becky was assured, be invaluable in their studies.

To die here, of hypothermia, would not be an unpleasant death she thought, if one could simply curl up on the ice. But for the explorers who died here, it was a very different story. One of pain and starvation and long endless days of untold misery as they struggled to survive.

'How do you feel about wildlife, Becky?' David Pollard's voice snapped her out of her trance.

'I love it. Why?'

'What do you think of this?'

He presented her with a skull. Becky took it and examined it closely.

'The teeth are absolutely amazing,' she said. 'All these tiny little barbs — what are they for?'

'It belonged to a Crabeater seal. The barbs as you call them are for straining out krill,' David explained. 'If you want to see a live one, there's a small group just beyond that hummock.'

'Really?'

She felt like a child, offered the sight of a litter of four week old puppies as she followed David across the ice.

The Crabeaters were on a floe some distance away, but it was a wonderful sight to behold.

'I'm taking the film unit in a bit closer,' David said.

'Is that a good idea?' Becky said, remembering what had happened to Simon when the ice parted beneath him.

'It's fine, I've okayed it with the boss,' David said. 'Want to come?'

'Well . . . '

'Go on,' Paul urged her. 'Come with us, Becky.'

'You can be our tea girl,' David added.

'You're on,' she said.

★　★　★

Where was she going now? It was hell being here on the ship with her prancing about on the ice like some kind of heroine in an old black and white movie. She was easy to spot, being so much smaller than anyone else. And now she was moving along with the film crew. Did those guys really know what they were doing out there? Was Alex aware that she was wandering off?

The weather was so good that when Alex and his team returned to the boat, it was only to pick up tents and camping gear.

'You're not seriously going to camp out on the ice?' Jake said as he watched them stow what they needed onto the Zodiac.

'It's firm, it's steady and the forecast is better than brilliant — yes, we're camping on the ice.'

'And Becky?'

Alex paused in what he was doing.

'You have a problem with that?'

Jake bristled. Sure he had a problem with it. It was true that you could see bad weather coming long before it hit, but if you weren't vigilant, if it crept up on you, no matter what the forecasts said they could find themselves in real danger out there — *she* could find herself in real danger.

'I'd just rather you were taking me along,' Jake said lamely.

'You'll get your chance,' Alex said, misunderstanding Jake's meaning.

He turned back to the task of loading supplies and Jake turned away. He'd never felt so helpless, and when he saw Becky hurrying towards them looking tiny and vulnerable wrapped in all that cold weather gear, he headed her off to the side.

'Don't try to talk me out of this,' she said.

'I'm not going to,' he said, unable to stop a smile at the way her chin shot up in that determined way of hers.

'Starting to see the bright side of having me out of your hair, huh?' she grinned impishly and the bristly defensiveness deserted her.

'Something like that,' he replied. 'You've got everything you need? Plenty of warm stuff. Make sure you eat well out there even if you don't feel hungry. And get as much rest as you can.'

She seemed to be ignoring him, delving around in her backpack.

'Callaghan, are you listening?'

She straightened up and held something out to him. A skull.

'David found this today — it belonged to one of those Crabeater seals you're so fond of. I thought you'd be interested in the teeth.'

He took it from her. A strange gift, but touching that she'd thought of him.

'You brought it back to show me,' he said.

'You don't mind, do you?' she said uncertainly. 'I really thought you'd — '

'Becky! Come on, we're moving out,' Alex called and she spun round.

Then she turned and looked over her shoulder at Jake and his breath was snatched away in an instant as she dazzled him with her smile.

'You don't have to keep it,' she said with a shrug. 'I'm sure someone else would like it if you don't. I won't be offended.'

'No, I'll . . . I'll keep it,' Jake said. 'Thanks, Becky. Take care out there.'

She looked at him for a moment, then she pulled her goggles down and hurried away from him.

He stood on the deck watching for a while, then returned to the sickbay. The skull needed a bit of cleaning up, but it was a fascinating object. She was right, he was interested. And once it was clean, he'd put it on a shelf — a slightly macabre ornament. But it was a reminder. A reminder that even out there, she had thought of him and she'd remembered his interest in the Crabeaters. He didn't like to admit even to himself just how much he was touched by that.

He barely slept while she was out camping on the ice.

They were gone for three days until a storm building up in the distance forced them back to the ship.

Becky could see Jake waiting on deck with some of the others, ready to help unload the Zodiac. He was scanning the faces on the Zodiac and when he found hers, he didn't look any further. She was so pleased to see him standing there, hands braced on the rail, long, strong legs slightly apart that she waved without thinking.

He waved back! This was crazy. Was it really possible that he was genuinely pleased to see her? And he was there on deck, grasping her wrist in a sailor's grip to help her aboard.

'Good time?' he asked as he took her bag from her.

'Brilliant,' she said. 'Cold, but fantastic. I got some great photos, Jake — I can rig my camera up to my laptop and show you later if you like.'

'Jake, hey!' Alex called. 'Where are you off to? Becky can carry her own bag back to the cabin. I need you here.'

Jake turned and smiled apologetically. 'See you later, maybe,' he said.

'Sure,' she took her bag back from him. It felt as if it weighed a ton.

Sleeping out on the ice had been a wonderful experience, but not a particularly comfortable one and she felt in dire need of a hot shower and a decent night's sleep in her own bunk.

And there was so much she wanted to tell Jake. So much to share with him about the past few days. After her shower she went to sickbay and there was the skull on a shelf. So he'd cleaned it up and kept it. That warmed her more than she thought possible.

8

Becky barely remembered getting ready for bed and when she woke the next morning, she saw a shadowy figure sitting at the desk, watching her. The light in the cabin was soft, coming from the light above the door and for a split second, she didn't recognise him.

She sat upright with a start and almost hit her head on the top bunk.

'Jake?' she cried. 'You nearly scared me to death. What are you doing in here? Is anything wrong?'

He turned the desk lamp on and smiled at her, but he didn't move from the chair. He had one ankle resting across his thigh and was leaning back, relaxed, comfortable.

'You didn't show up for breakfast,' he said. 'I was worried about you.'

She looked at the clock. 'Is that the time? How could I sleep in? I must have slept right through my alarm.'

'I brought you breakfast,' he went on. 'But it's cold now.'

'Jake,' she whispered, frowning. 'How long have you been sitting there, watching me sleep?'

'Long enough,' he said, uncrossing his legs and leaning forward. 'You looked so untroubled, so peaceful. I didn't want to disturb you. Watching someone sleep can be very soothing. I'll go and get you a fresh coffee and see if I can rustle up some food.'

'Coffee would be good,' she said gratefully. 'But no food. It's almost lunchtime already.'

'Back soon,' he said, closing the door with a quiet click behind him.

Becky leaned back against the wall for a moment, then swung her legs off the bunk and headed for the shower.

She'd missed this out on the ice. The invigorating hot needles of water pounding her body. By the time he returned with coffee, she was dressed.

'Sorry I took so long,' he said with an

almost rueful smile.

He put the coffee down on the table.

'Why Callaghan?' he asked.

'Sorry?' Her heart jumped and began to beat faster. She pretended not to understand the question, but she knew perfectly well what he meant.

'Why the name change?' he went on. 'When I asked about where your husband fitted in to all this, you said it was complicated.'

Her face burned. She remembered — he hadn't given her chance to answer. She longed to tell him and often wondered about how she would do it, but now he really was giving her the opportunity to put things straight.

She moved closer to him and sat on the other chair facing him.

'You really want to know?' she asked.

'I wouldn't ask if I didn't. We can't deny there's something between us.'

He reached out and took hold of her hand and his touch was like an electric charge to her skin.

'I don't think there is a marriage any

more, is there?' he went on.

'No,' she dropped her head. Her throat felt tight, as if it was closing up and tears pricked her eyelids. The moment of truth as they called it. The point of no return, for once she told him, there would be no going back.

'The truth can't be any worse than a wrong assumption,' he said, his voice achingly gentle.

She looked up at him, her violet eyes dark with sorrow.

'Don't you believe it,' she said hoarsely. She'd fought so hard to keep this from him and now she wanted the truth out once and for all. 'I'm a widow, Jake. My husband, Bryn, is dead.'

She looked down again, but heard him suck in his breath harshly and dragged her eyes back up, forcing herself to look at him, ready to face the anger and accusation she felt sure would be in his eyes, fearing it, but as prepared as she'd ever be. But there was no anger, just surprise, as if he'd expected to hear almost anything but that.

He was silent for a moment. 'And all that talk before,' he said after what seemed to Becky like an eternity. 'Was a cover to hide your distress.'

She squeezed his hand back, drawing strength from him, so much comfort from the simple act of holding hands. She bit back tears.

'Was it an accident?' Jake asked gently.

'No. My husband had a grade II Anaplastic Astrocytoma. Because of the location of the tumour, surgery was never an option. He went through radiation therapy and chemotherapy. It took several months for him to die.'

She was aware of her voice trembling slightly as she tried to relay the facts. Despite everything, she was haunted by Bryn's decline. She could still see the fear in his eyes as they were told of the diagnosis. She could almost feel his hand gripping her arm like a claw.

Back then he'd had the strength to

bruise her, but she'd been oblivious to pain. He hadn't borne his illness bravely or with good humour. The poor guy had been terrified out of his mind every step of the way, clinging to her, draining her and she'd had to remain strong enough for both of them.

'He . . . ' she began, but her voice failed her and when she closed her eyes, she felt Jake's arms fold around her and pull her towards him, taking her onto his lap and cradling her like a child.

She rested her head against his solid, warm chest and listened to the hard, steady beat of his heart as he folded his arms around her and held her close. Was that heart big enough to handle everything she had to tell him?

'Oh, Becky,' his voice cracked. 'Why didn't you tell me? Is that why you didn't want to see me again, because your grief was still so fresh.'

'You don't understand, Jake,' she said brokenly. 'On the night I came to your apartment, my husband was still alive. But only just.'

She watched his eyes narrow and prepared herself for a backlash of anger and even winced as she anticipated the explosion to come.

'Didn't you hear what I said, Jake?' she almost sobbed, struggling to free herself from his embrace. 'I left my dying husband in a hospice and came to you. What does that tell you about me?'

'It says more about me than it does about you,' he murmured. 'It says I've been too busy licking my own wounds to see yours. I've been an idiot, Becky. I'm not going to ask your forgiveness because I don't deserve it after the way I've behaved.'

This time he couldn't stop her breaking free.

'Stop it, Jake! I don't want your sympathy,' she cried angrily. 'I could cope better with your anger than I can with this. You don't know the half of it! You just don't know!'

The last was said with such despair, the words torn from her with such bitterness. She thought she'd got rid of all that, had shaken it off, lost it out there somewhere on the ice among the blue shadows and screeching birds.

'Then tell me, Becky,' he said gently.

She looked across at him.

Slumping down on the bunk she shook her head. Tell him the rest? Tell him how her own husband had rejected her so soon after their marriage? See that look of pity in his eyes deepen and intensify?

He moved towards her and she didn't resist when he pulled her into his arms again. 'I can understand why you wouldn't want to talk to me,' he said. 'And I'm not going to push you. Not now. Not ever. If you want to tell me the rest of it, then I'll listen. Trust me, Becky. We were good friends before any of this happened — we can be again.'

Wasn't that why she'd gone to him in the first place? Because she trusted him, because he was her friend? But she hadn't trusted him enough to be honest with him. If only she had.

'Let's not go to the mess for lunch,' he said. 'You clear off the desk and I'll bring food back here. God knows, it would be nice to have a little peace and privacy for a meal without listening to them all talking about the Antarctic Biome.'

The idea appealed. Becky nodded. She didn't feel like facing anyone else right now, but she was hungry. Emotionally she felt wrung out.

The love she felt for Jake and the harsh reality of Bryn's deception and death churned inside her, a strange mixture of almost euphoric happiness and agonising sadness.

'All right?' he asked, squeezing her hands. 'I won't be long.'

She waited until he'd gone before standing up and clearing off the desk.

Jake hurried back to the cabin with a metal tray loaded with food, his thoughts in utter chaos. He tapped the door with his foot and Becky opened it, smiling wanly up at him.

So pale, so dark eyed — the violet

irises almost purple with sorrow, and yet still so beautiful.

'It's nice to sit together to eat,' he said, unloading the tray onto the desk.

Her hands shook when she picked up her knife and fork. He longed to reach out and steady them, but there was lost ground to cover and a sense of having to get to know each other all over again.

She didn't eat much in the end.

'I'm very tired,' she said apologetically as she pushed her plate away.

'You didn't have breakfast,' he reminded her. 'You should eat, Becky.'

Nevertheless, he collected up their plates and stacked them on the tray.

'You've had a busy few days,' he said. 'I'll take these back to the galley and I'll probably watch a film or something with the guys. You get a shower and try to rest this afternoon and I'll see you in the morning.'

She hadn't come to him that night because she wanted him, but because she needed a shoulder to cry on. He couldn't have got it more wrong, and the last thing she needed now was him treating her as anything other than just a friend.

'Can I get you anything else?' he asked, resting his hand on her shoulder and squeezing lightly.

She looked up at him, then to his surprise reached up and covered his hand with her own. Her palm felt icy cold.

'No, thank you,' she smiled softly. 'I'll see you later, perhaps. You should get some rest too if you can. Alex was saying he expects the weather to clear again soon and you'll be out on the ice next time.'

* * *

When he'd gone, Becky wept. She wept for poor Bryn whose life had drained away like water from a dripping tap. She wept for herself, sitting faithfully at his bedside, cleaning him up when he'd been so sick after chemotherapy, holding him when he sobbed because he'd woken up to find a clump of hair on his pillow.

And then there was Elizabeth. She couldn't even bring herself to hate her, but Becky knew that Elizabeth wouldn't be scarred by Bryn's illness and death the same way she was. She'd almost seemed to enjoy being there at the end in some weird, perverse way.

But most of all, she wept for Jake. Dear, honest, sweet, Jake who she had used and hurt and rejected in the cruellest way possible. Whatever he might say, would he ever really be able to forgive her for that — deep down where it mattered?

Alex said Jake's ex-wife had betrayed him. That sort of pain went deep and Becky wasn't sure if it would ever go away.

She grabbed a handful of tissues and sat down in front of the mirror.

Casualties of love, that's what they were. But were they curable? That was the big question. Could broken hearts be mended?

Endless days of gales and blizzards followed. Seasickness was a problem for some of the men, but even the worst affected seemed to acclimatise.

Jake and Becky were kept moderately busy helping out with experiments on board ship or playing cards with some of the guys.

A few days later they woke to a clear day and as Becky had predicted, it was Jake's turn out on the ice. It was over a week before Jake and Becky were back on the ship together again.

When the sunrise came, cheers and a noticeable lifting of spirits greeted its arrival. And after that, things got really busy and the pace of life on board ship stepped up a notch. Not so much for Becky and Jake, who always seemed somewhat surplus to requirements on trips to the pack, but for the scientists and film crew.

Spring came quickly after that and Alex announced that they'd soon be moving away from the pack ice and winding up the trip. But on the day they were to move, David spotted Weddell Seal pups and it was decided to venture onto the ice one last time so that he could film them.

'Becky or Jake?' Alex asked, a mischievous twinkle in his eye. 'Who is it to be? You've both had equal time on these trips. Shall we toss for it?'

'No need,' Jake said. 'Becky can take this one if she wants it. I've seen enough seals, penguins and ice to last a lifetime.'

'Well, Becky?' Alex turned to her. 'What do you say?'

'If Jake's sure,' she said. 'I'd love one more chance to go on the ice.'

She'd love one more chance full stop. However kind Jake was towards her, she knew that deep down there was no future for them. Since the day she'd told him about Bryn, he seemed to avoid being alone with her.

There were more in the shore party than usual Becky noted as they squeezed into the Zodiac and, as always, Jake stood on the deck leaning on the rail watching them as they moved off.

Was he just giving her space to sort her feelings out? Was he the one that needed space and time? She just didn't know. And soon this trip would be over and they'd go their separate ways and that thought brought a chill to her heart far colder than anything the Antarctic could produce.

Thank God this would soon be over, Jake thought as the Zodiac sped towards the Weddell Seals. Every time she went onto the ice, he felt on edge. So much could happen out there. So much could go wrong.

He'd carefully avoided being on his own with Becky over the past few weeks. He didn't trust himself with her. She was still vulnerable.

She needed time to grieve properly, to mourn her husband.

He was still bothered by that night, but more bothered now by his own part in it. She'd come to him in despair and he was the one who'd got hold of the wrong end of the stick.

He wanted to get back to work, to doing what he did best and apart from the occasional mild case of frostnip and a couple of cases of food poisoning, he'd had little to do.

Becky returned from her last time on the ice exhilarated and rosy cheeked. The pups had been gorgeous and so easy to observe. It didn't matter that they were the most easily studied of the seals; it took none of the magic away from her.

She wanted to find Jake and tell him all about it, like an excited child after a trip to the zoo eager to share her experiences. He was the one person on earth she wanted to see right now.

But before eating and before looking for Jake, Becky went to her cabin to change her clothes and brush her hair and stood in front of the mirror cursing the fact that she hadn't brought any make up along. There had to be some way of making Jake take notice of her again, to get him to stop treading on eggshells whenever he was near.

But how could she let him know how she felt without having him thinking she was hurling herself at him?

The door opened suddenly, hitting her and knocking her into the cabin. She spun round and there was Jake, his hands reaching to steady her, only letting go once he was sure she was steady.

'There you are,' he said. 'Come with me, Callaghan.'

'What?'

'You heard me,' he laughed. 'Quickly, or you'll miss it and I don't want you to miss this.'

'What? Why?'

'Stop asking questions,' he said, still smiling as he reached out his hand to her. 'Come on, this may not last.'

She pulled her hand away suspiciously.

'This isn't one of those end of trip rituals is it? I'm not going to end up on my head in a barrel of water or something am I?'

Jake roared with laughter. 'You will if you don't stop wasting time,' he said. 'Come on! This is important. Please, Becky. I just want to show you something outside, something remarkable. It's a once in a lifetime opportunity and I want you to see it.'

'I've just come in from outside,' she said, puzzled. 'I've only been back on board a few minutes.'

'But you didn't see it?'

'See what?'

He laughed. 'If you had, then you'd know what I was talking about. Come on,' he reached out his hand. 'Trust me.'

Trust him? Oh, if only he would trust her.

She put her hand in his and followed him out into the corridor.

Others were heading for the deck too, their voices an excited babble.

Jake was moving fast and she had to run to keep up with him, then he was opening the door and they were back out on deck. Her foot slipped and he caught her round the waist, holding her steady as they moved across towards the rail.

'Look,' he said, his arm still around her.

She didn't want to look. She was enjoying the warmth of his arm held tightly around her, the sudden surprising closeness of him that seemed to come so naturally. She looked up at him, but his eyes were sparkling as he gazed at something in the distance.

Everyone else who had come out to the deck had fallen silent. There was a sense of awe over the whole ship's company.

Becky followed Jake's gaze across the water. The edge of the ice pack was breaking up now and . . . she did a double take and Jake gave her a squeeze, instinctively knowing the moment she saw it. 'How about that?' he breathed almost reverently as if speaking in anything above a whisper might dispel the vision before them completely.

Becky was captivated, enchanted even.

Before her she could see columns of ice rising up in the distance where before it had been relatively flat. She blinked but the image remained and it looked to her like some kind of mystical, magical castle sparkling and shining. It even appeared to have towers and turrets.

'It looks like some sort of ice palace,' she said. 'Is it an iceberg?'

'No,' he said. 'It's a Fata Morgana — a mirage.'

She leaned against him without even thinking about it and stared into the distance. How could something that wasn't there look so real, so completely solid? She felt almost as if she could walk across the ice and step right inside the crystal walls.

Jake kept his arm tightly around her and it seemed the most natural thing in the world to slide her own arm around him.

'You know why it's called a Fata Morgana?' he asked softly. 'It's Italian for Fairy Morgana who was King Arthur's half-sister. A dangerous woman, deceptive, manipulative — a seductive enchantress.'

Becky pulled away from him a little. His words bit deep.

'Abandoned and betrayed by the men she loved,' she murmured. 'Misunderstood and much-maligned.'

'Perhaps she was,' Jake said and he looked down at Becky with such warmth in his eyes that she felt she might melt. She had the feeling that neither of them was talking about Morgana, but about Becky herself.

Hadn't Jake thought she was manipulative? A seductress? Perhaps not any more, but he had once. And didn't she feel she'd been misunderstood and much-maligned?

'Who are we to judge what she may or may not have been?' Jake asked. 'It's the stuff of legends. She was beautiful, we can probably be sure of that much, but her character has been interpreted differently over the years. Who knows what kind of person life made her?'

Becky wondered what kind of person her own life had made of her. Was she really going to let her failed marriage to Bryn taint the rest of her life?

'Are you in there, Morgan Le Fay?' Jake murmured and it was so real that Becky would not have been surprised to see the mythical woman emerge from the palace and glide across the ice towards them.

'Wasn't she said to have lived in a crystal palace under the sea?' Becky asked, recalling the legend.

'And she could build castles out of thin air,' Jake replied so lightly that she barely heard him.

Their eyes met and Becky saw nothing but love reflected in his. She looked away quickly, confused. It was the magic of the moment, that was all. She'd be a fool to read anything more into it.

The illusion shimmered before them looking every bit as real as the surrounding ice and yet as unreal as a dream.

'To be scientific about it,' Jake went on. 'It's a layer of warm air lying over the cold surface which bends the light and makes it appear to rise vertically. A simple phenomena and quite common down here, but rarely as spectacular as this.'

'I think I prefer to think it's Morgan Le Fay's crystal palace,' Becky said. 'It's far too beautiful to be explained by science.'

'I won't argue with that,' Jake said and she rested her head against him and felt him breathe a contented sigh. If only they could have shifted reality, swept away the past, Becky could have stayed like that forever.

They stood out on the deck for what seemed an eternity until the light changed and the ice palace vanished. For a while, everything else had slipped into insignificance. Becky's thoughts and feelings had stopped tumbling around her head and she'd felt truly at peace.

Now she felt the cold that had seeped deep into the very marrow of her bones and, as reality bit home, she turned to look up at Jake.

'I'm looking forward to going home,' Jake said as they headed back inside. 'I've never been down here in winter before, by the way. Last time I came it was all day sunshine, with just wall to wall penguins and the occasional whale.'

'You're bored?' she said as they made their way back to the cabin.

'I'm not bored,' he said. 'I'm going out of my mind. To come here from a busy — scrub that, frantic, emergency department and find myself twiddling my thumbs all day every day is driving me crazy.'

No way did she wish for casualties or for anyone to be hurt, but when you were used to rushing from one patient to another, having next to nothing to do apart from stick on the occasional plaster was seriously weird.

'The last trip I did with Alex wasn't

as well funded as this,' Jake said. 'I had to do a lot of work, but on this trip I feel like a tourist.'

They'd arrived back at the cabin. It was time to get rid of the outdoor gear and go along to the mess for dinner.

'Well, I expect Simon was glad you were along,' she pointed out as he helped her off with her jacket. His hands brushed against her neck and she shivered, but he didn't seem to notice.

'Alex was there if I hadn't been,' he said. He was looking at her strangely. Deeply. As if he could see right inside her.

'How are we going to cope with this?' he asked. 'We can't deny the physical attraction between us. I ache for you. It's taken every ounce of my willpower to stay in that sickbay and not to come knocking on your door.'

Physical attraction? Was that all it was?

'And it would be so wrong,' he went on.

Wrong. Yes. Of course it would be

wrong. She wasn't the sort of woman he wanted to get hooked up with, was she? Becky thought bitterly.

'We'll cope,' she said briskly. 'It won't be for much longer.'

'Cope?' he breathed. 'I don't know if I can. Come on, let's eat.'

Sitting down, eating, things felt much easier, but Becky was all too aware every time Jake's leg brushed her leg, or his hand touched hers as he reached for the water jug. Electricity sparked between them.

'Anything planned when we get home?' he asked. 'Got a job lined up?'

She smiled. 'I may go back to City. You?'

He shrugged. 'I haven't decided yet, although Douglas did tell me he'd keep my job open.'

'He told me that too,' Becky said incredulously. 'You mean to tell me he's operating that department with locums — just in case we decide to come back?'

Jake grinned. 'He must think a lot of us both,' he said. 'And we weren't solely the department, Becky. There are others.'

'Do you think you'll go back?'

'Who knows,' he said and Becky wondered if it would depend on her.

He didn't love her. What he felt was physical attraction. But she loved him, loved him with all her heart and soul and she knew she couldn't work beside him every day knowing he would never return her feelings.

'About Thalia,' Becky began.

'What about her?'

He didn't look shocked or surprised to hear his ex-wife's name mentioned. 'What happened?'

'She left me.'

'I'm sorry,' she wished she hadn't asked.

'I'm not,' he said. 'Look, Thalia and I were young when we married. It wasn't real. It wasn't her leaving me that hurt, but the way she did it — with someone else. I was working hard, didn't have a clue. But you get over it, you move on, you stop thinking that you're in some way a failure as a person. At least I did.'

She cleared her throat. Perhaps now was as good a time as any to tell him the rest of her story.

'Bryn left me too,' she admitted. 'More than once. The last time was for Elizabeth. I took him back when the brain tumour was diagnosed.'

Jake swore under his breath. 'And Elizabeth?'

'Didn't want to know until the end,' Becky shrugged. 'Waltzed into the hospice, flung her coat down, took hold of his hand and prepared to play the grieving mistress making it clear I was surplus to requirements.'

'Let me guess,' Jake murmured. 'You came straight to see me, but needed courage, so you went along to the wine bar and had a couple of drinks first.'

'More than a couple,' she smiled at him over the rim of her water glass.

'Becky . . . don't you know? Nothing happened that night,' he said. 'You fell asleep and I put you to bed and went to sleep on the sofa.'

'Really?' she gasped.

'Yes,' he smiled. 'Really.'

She bit her lip. So all this time she'd been beating herself up about her behaviour and nothing had happened. Jake had been a perfect gentleman — luckily for her.

'I . . . I think I might go to bed now,' she said.

'Good idea. See you in the morning, Callaghan,' he said.

9

Jake sat through a movie that evening, staring at the screen, but taking nothing in. He had to stop trying to push himself at Becky. Hell, she might not even want him, but those weren't the signals she was giving out.

But he wanted more, so much more than to be a shoulder for her to cry on. He wanted more than to be a release for her pain. He wanted her love. But how could she love anyone after all she'd been through with Bryn? Their marriage, his betrayal and then his death.

He knew how it felt to be rejected in favour of someone else. To say it shattered the confidence was an understatement.

It was possible to love again — and deeper. His feelings for Becky were stronger, more powerful, more real than anything in his life before.

Gradually the mess emptied and the men returned to their cabins until Jake was sitting alone.

The atmosphere on board ship the next day was like that at the end of a school trip. Everyone a little excited and happy to be going home, but at the same time, sad to be leaving.

'Fancy a walk?' Jake murmured, his lips so close to her ear that Becky could feel the warmth of his breath. 'A last stroll on deck before the bad weather sets in?'

She nodded, the lump in her throat making a spoken reply impossible.

They stepped out into the corridor as Alex was coming their way.

'I've got some bad news,' Alex said. 'We're staying put for the next few hours. There's a storm heading our way and we'll wait until the worst is over before we get underway.'

He lowered his head and started to duck through the dooreway, but then backed up into the corridor and looked at them both again questioningly.

'Where are you two off to?'

'We're going for a walk round deck,' Jake said.

'Make it brief,' Alex said. 'That storm is closing in fast.' Then his face broke into a smile. 'Won't be much longer, though, and we'll be back on dry land again.'

Somehow that thought brought little comfort to Becky.

'Hold on to me,' Jake said as they stepped out into the teeth of a roaring gale and Becky grasped his arm to steady herself.

The blizzard had come upon them fast. Snow wasn't falling, but was being whipped up from the surface by the wind creating blinding conditions. Visibility was reducing by the second and the ice pack was almost invisible. It was a struggle to get as far as the rail and when they reached it, they clung on.

So much for a pleasant stroll around the deck.

'I didn't realise it would be as bad as

this,' Jake shouted above the raging wind. 'Shall we . . . '

He started to turn back, then stopped.

'Becky!' he shouted. 'Do you see that?'

She scrunched her eyes, tried to see through the driving snow, but could only make out shadows moving on the pack. Dim, distant shadows.

'Seals?' she said. 'Penguins?'

'Too big,' he grasped the rail and leaned forward as if an extra inch or two would make any difference. 'It can't be, that's impossible . . . Becky, those are people out there.'

As he said it, it made sense. People shapes. But how? There weren't any other boats in the vicinity. And now they were gone, lost in the white.

'Come on,' he grabbed her hand and struggled back inside, bowing his head down against the wind and bolting the door behind them.

'Are you sure, Jake?' Becky asked as they shook the snow off themselves and ran down the corridor towards the sickbay.

'They were people,' he said. 'I know it. You saw them.'

'I saw something,' she admitted. 'But people? That's impossible, Jake.'

'I know what I saw,' he said. 'It wasn't a mirage. It was real. And they're going to need help.'

'Who needs help?' Alex asked.

'I saw a group of people on the pack,' Jake said, irritated, and Alex rose slowly to his feet.

'You can hardly see the pack,' Alex said. 'You probably saw some wildlife. You know how things get distorted down here.'

Becky noticed Jake clenching his fists at his sides.

'I know what I saw,' he said. 'Becky was there. She saw them too.'

Alex turned his eyes to Becky. 'Did you?'

'I did see something,' she said. 'I suppose it could have been people.'

Alex laughed. 'There are no other

people for miles around,' he said. 'You probably saw some seals.'

'Look, I know what I saw,' Jake said, his eyes glittering fiercely. 'And if you won't come with me, I'll take the damn Zodiac to the pack on my own and see for myself.'

Becky looked from one to the other.

'They were heading for our lights, Alex. Looking for safety.'

'If there are people out there,' Becky said. 'We need to be prepared. We'll need warm IV fluid.'

'If you're wrong . . . ' Alex began. 'The consequences . . . '

'And the consequences if I'm right and we ignore what I know I saw?' Jake replied.

They stared at each other for a moment, then Alex strode purposefully towards the door.

'I'll get a team together. We'll check this out, but quickly. I'm not risking lives out there unnecessarily and if we don't find anything straight away, we come straight back, okay? This storm will get worse before it gets better and I don't want to be stuck out there in it.'

In the sickbay Jake saw Becky preparing two shore packs.

'I won't need two,' he said. 'The priority will be to get those people on board as quickly as possible.'

'One each,' Becky said. 'For you and me. If something happens and we can't get back to the Delphinus, then we'll need to be prepared to treat them in the field.'

'So you do believe me,' he said, his face softening.

'I know you, Jake. You wouldn't risk lives on a what if or maybe. And you'll let me come along?'

'I wouldn't dream of stopping you,' he said, eyes creasing with warmth. 'Besides, I prefer to have you along. If we do end up having to treat casualties on the ice, I'll need you there. Dress warmly, Becky, don't leave any part of yourself vulnerable.'

'You too,' she said and their eyes

locked briefly. They both knew how dangerous this could be.

Alex went to assemble a small team of his most experienced men to go in the Zodiac while Jake had got his qualified first aiders briefed and ready for their return in sickbay.

When Jake and Becky arrived in the mess, Alex was giving a briefing.

'We'll be roped together,' Alex explained. 'All of us. There'll be no stragglers, no heroes, okay? We work as a team. It really is all for one and one for all out there in those conditions. Understood?'

No one questioned what Jake had seen.

'We're going to take the Delphinus as close to the pack as we can,' Alex went on. 'I don't want to risk breaking the ice near those people, but I want to have the ship as close as humanly possible. Remember, visibility will be zero out there. Okay. Ready? Let's get on deck and start to acclimatise ourselves to these conditions.'

The deck was icy and covered in snow and the sea was heaving. Jake put his arm around Becky's waist and held her close.

'I'm not letting you out of my sight,' he said.

And he didn't. Jake kept Becky as close to him as it was possible in the Zodiac as it approached the pack.

Someone had joked that what Jake had seen may have been ghosts. But he knew what he saw and quite apart from the fact that they shouldn't have been there, there was something about the shambling, shuffling shapes that rang alarm bells. There had been a look of pure desperation about them.

He had learned to trust his instincts and they'd never let him down yet.

They reached the pack and everyone safely exited the Zodiac.

Thank God the wind wasn't as bad as it could have been, but the visibility could hardly have been worse.

Becky suddenly seemed smaller and out there on the ice, where you couldn't see your hand in front of your face, Jake was terrified of losing her.

But they were roped together and as long as he could feel the tension on the rope, he knew she was close behind him, but still he had to keep looking over his shoulder to see for himself her small, dark shape following along behind him.

'Where?' Alex yelled.

'Around here somewhere,' Jake said, the first tendrils of uncertainty beginning to snake around his confidence. 'This area.'

Out here everything looked the same — what they could see of it. And now he didn't even know which direction the ship was in — couldn't even make out the lights through the snow.

If he'd brought Becky out here on a wild goose chase, risked her neck as well as everyone else's . . . Then he turned and saw the dim gleam of light from the ship and suddenly he had his bearings again and the despair that had clouded him suddenly lifted.

'This way,' he shouted, striding forward.

Jake peered and squinted into the snow, but there was no sign of any life at all and he knew that the worst thing about never finding the people he'd seen would be knowing they must have perished or been lost.

He looked over his shoulder at Becky. She was just a dark shape smothered in white trudging along behind, but she meant the world to him.

She should have stayed on board. There was no way they were treating anyone out here in the field. The weather was too bad and without any kind of shelter, any kind of treatment would be impossible.

Walking against the wind was exhausting and now the lights of the Delphinus were lost.

Alex who was leading the party turned and walked back to Jake.

'I'm sorry,' he began. 'I'm calling an

end to this now.'

Becky could feel Jake's disappoint-ment and despondency as something tangible, as if the rope holding them together was acting as some kind of conduit between them.

'You can't give up!' she shouted. 'We simly can't turn back now. We've come this far.'

And then she rubbed the snow from her goggles and looked round. All she could see were a group of seals huddled down, sheltering by a hummock, their dark shapes barely visible. Realisation bit.

'Over there!'

The dark, huddled shapes had vanished and Becky began to wonder if she'd seen anything at all, but Jake wasn't waiting for a second chance.

'Come on!' he yelled. 'Where, Becky? Exactly?'

'That way,' she said with utter certainty, driving her fist in the direction that she'd seen the men. Because she knew beyond any shred of doubt that they were men and they were in trouble. Jake had been right and she had been right to believe him.

They stumbled and ran where Becky had told them.

The wind seemed to draw back, hold its breath and suddenly the window in the snow was open again and the shapes were visible. Closer now, darker, bigger.

Six men. Six exhausted, soaking wet, drained and hurting men, but they raised a weak cheer when they saw the party from the Delphinus approaching and Becky felt her heart constrict inside her chest.

They would be desperate for warmth, but to warm them here and now would be dangerous. Safer for them to walk on painfully frost-bitten feet than to make any attempt at rewarming only to risk them freezing again.

Two of the men couldn't stand. The other four were able to stand, but with great difficulty. The team from the Delphinus surrounded them, roping them together and lifting the two worst cases off the ice.

'Are there just six of you?' Jake said. 'Six? You're all here?'

'Seven. There were seven of us.'

Becky saw Jake straighten up and look around. She knew what he was thinking even as he started unfastening the rope.

'Don't even think about it,' she said, pounding her fist against his padded arm. 'Alex said no heroics, remember? We work as a team.'

'You heard what he said,' Jake replied. 'There's another one of them out here somewhere.'

'Yes, I heard, but we'll all look for him,' Becky said with determination.

'Her,' the guy shouted wearily. 'Her name's Jan. She's dead. We had no choice but to leave her.'

'Where?'

When they finally found her her body was completely covered in snow.

But she deserved a more dignified end than this. Those poor guys had been carrying her for days. Becky couldn't begin to imagine how hard the decision to leave her must have been for them.

Jake brushed the snow away from her body and then lifted her up easily into his arms.

'Not dead,' he said and once again, Becky had no reason to doubt him.

Alex did a head count. 'We're twenty minutes away from the Zodiac,' he yelled. 'We need to move fast before this gets worse.'

Worse? Could it get any worse? Becky knew the answer to that. Yes, of course it could, it could get much, much worse.

Going back, one of the men they'd rescued fell and took Becky down with him. At once, Jake was lifting her back to her feet with just one strong hand, still holding the apparently dead woman in his arms.

'All right?' he asked.

'Yes,' she said. 'Keep going!'

Jake squeezed her arm and she knew

he was smiling at her, even though she couldn't see his face, could barely even see him. She smiled back. He adjusted the woman's weight in his arms and trudged onwards.

★ ★ ★

'No pulse, no breath,' Becky said. 'This doesn't look good, Jake.'

But Jake was already working on Jan.

'Not dead until warm and dead,' Jake reminded her of the cold-weather maxim. 'I'm not giving up on her yet.'

'I'm glad to hear it,' Becky smiled. 'What do you want me to do?'

'Pull the curtain round, Becky,' he said softly. 'Let's give her some dignity and get Alex to come in here. I'd rather have you assist me, but those other two guys need your help.'

She nodded and pulled the curtains round the bed.

They were back on board the Delphinus, safe in the sickbay with the raging blizzard just muted background noise.

The two men who had been unable to walk were suffering from severe frostbite. Their feet were hard, white and had all the appearance of frozen poultry. The other four were just cold and exhausted.

Luke was immediately on hand to help out and he had already warmed bowls of water.

'Forty-two degrees, Becky,' he said. 'Precisely.'

'Great,' Becky said. 'Heibler jackets on all of them, please. David, bring in warm, sweet drinks and Ray, set them up with warm, moist oxygen, forty-two degrees at mask.'

She turned her attention to the two men who were in the worst shape. 'You don't need me to tell you that your feet are frozen solid. I'm going to immerse them in warm water for twenty minutes and it's going to be painful when sensation returns, so I'll give you painkillers immediately.'

'Alex! She's in VF,' Jake's voice came to her. 'Get Becky in here, now!'

'Feet in the bowls,' Becky said. 'Twenty minutes only. Don't rub your feet whatever you do . . .'

She rushed behind the curtain where Jake was ready with the paddles.

'Becky — can you do the honours?'

'I — I'm sorry,' Alex stuttered. 'I — I don't . . .'

'It's all right, Alex,' Jake said as Becky moved over to control the defibrillator. 'Becky . . . ready? Charge . . . clear!'

He placed the paddles and an electric charge jolted through Jan's body.

Becky looked at the monitor. 'Still in VF.'

'Again,' Jake said. 'Ready? Charge . . . clear!'

Once again he placed the paddles and this time the monitor showed a rhythm. Jake's tired, but satisfied smile was a picture.

'Thanks, Becky,' he said. 'And Alex. Sorry I yelled.'

'Do you need me any more?' Becky asked, eager to get back to the men she was treating.

'I'll always need you,' Jake murmured so softly that Becky wasn't even sure that was what he said. Then he snapped his attention back to the job in hand and added, 'I'll give you a shout if I do — you likewise, if you come across any problems.'

Becky stepped out from behind the curtain to find a sea of anxious faces looking at her.

'Does that mean she's not dead?' someone asked, looking all at once stricken and delighted. 'Did we leave her to die?'

'You didn't leave her to die,' Becky said. 'If we hadn't come along, there was nothing you could have done to save her. And she wouldn't have known anything about it. But no, she's not dead. Far from it.'

The long, laborious process of literally defrosting the tissue had only just begun. Even when the temperature was up to normal, the men would have to endure severe swelling over the next few hours and blistering within the next two days.

She moved on to the next guy, Adrian, who seemed to be in charge.

He pulled the oxygen mask away from his face.

'Is this necessary?' he asked. 'All this?'

'You know it is,' she said. 'How long were you out on the ice?'

'Two weeks.'

'Two weeks?' Becky gasped. 'You were lost all that time? What happened? We hadn't been notified of anyone lost in the area.'

Alex came over and joined her.

'That's because no one knew we were,' Adrian sighed. 'We lost our boat and just managed to abandon ship before she sank taking all our radio equipment and most of our gear with her. We couldn't afford to charter an ice breaker like this.'

'Next time,' Alex said. 'Try to get a place on a large vessel. We're not just one expedition on here.'

'Next time?' Adrian said, looking as if wild horses wouldn't drag him down here again, but Becky knew he would change his mind. The place would lure him back eventually.

'You were lucky,' Alex said. 'We're getting underway now though. I want to get you all to shore and to a proper hospital.'

10

Becky looked around the sickbay. It had been a very long night indeed but finally the initial energency was over and in the quiet they had a moment to sit and take stock.

'There's no need for us both to be up all night,' Jake whispered. 'I can keep an eye on things here.'

'I don't feel tired,' she lied. She felt dead on her feet, but she didn't want to go back to the cabin, alone. She wanted to stay with Jake because in a couple of days they would be back in South America and suddenly the whole thing would be over.

Jake placed his thumb under her chin and tilted her face.

'You look exhausted,' he said gently.

His eyes found hers, blue and gold and beautiful.

'I know you were hurting,' he said at

last, his voice tender and sweet. 'I know you came looking for a shoulder to cry on and I misunderstood. And then I got you all wrong and treated you so badly. I just . . . I want you to know that I'll always be here for you.'

'But only as a shoulder to cry on?' she asked, suddenly shaky.

He was telling her in the kindest way possible that he wanted to be her friend, nothing more. She knew that. He couldn't love her. Not after what she'd done.

★　★　★

Becky woke feeling wonderfully rested. She stretched and smiled. Her whole body felt terrific, but then reality crashed in and she sat upright with a start and she realised someone was knocking on the door.

'Come in,' she said sleepily.

Alex poked his head round the door. 'Morning,' he said.

'What's the time?' she said. 'Why

didn't anyone wake me, I should . . . '

'You needed the rest,' Alex grinned. 'We're here — Ushuaia.'

'Jake?'

'Gone,' Alex said. 'He went to the hospital with the casualties.'

'So what do I do now?' Becky asked, for the first time in her life unsure of what her next step should be. 'Where do I go?'

'Home,' Alex beamed. 'It's where we're all headed.'

So it really was all over now.

'We won't all get on flights together of course,' Alex went on. 'But some of the guys are planning to stay in Buenos Aires for a few days anyway. What are you going to do, Becky?'

'I — I don't know,' she said.

She couldn't believe Jake had gone without even saying goodbye.

★   ★   ★

She went with some of the others to Ezeiza International Airport.

Once she'd got herself booked on a flight, she planned to sit on a chair and sleep for however long it took. Hours, days — what did it matter?

Jake had been busy, caught up in caring for the casualties. He had fully intended to return to the Delphinus to see Becky before she left, but by the time he got back there, she'd already gone as if she couldn't wait to get away from the place — and him.

He stared out of the window at a blanket of cloud stretching out as far as the eye could see and closed his eyes. It would be so nice to be able to sleep all the way home.

Becky turned to the guy sitting beside her on the plane.

'Would you excuse me, please?' she asked politely. 'I'm afraid I need to go to the bathroom.'

She needed to be somewhere private and alone to try to gain some control over the misery that kept rising up in overwhelming waves.

'Sure,' he said.

She started towards the toilets, looking at the faces of the other passengers, but not really seeing them. Then she saw him and every other passenger on the plane ceased to exist.

He was leaning back, his eyes closed, his eyelashes a dark sweep against his face. How could this be? The two of them on the same plane? She hadn't seen him at the airport. But she'd been one of the first to board the plane and if he'd come along at the last minute . . .

Jake's eyes opened, looking right at her, startlingly blue. It made her jump. Her eyes widened as he began to rise in his seat.

'Becky . . . ' he said her name. She took off, hurrying towards the toilet, but he caught up with her.

And now he was beside her, looming over her, looking down at her, his hand gripping her upper arm.

'Why did you run away?' he asked.

'I . . . I needed to get to the . . . '

'Not just now,' he hissed. 'In Ushuaia. I got back to the boat and looked for you, but you'd gone.'

She blinked as his words sunk in.

'Back to . . . but I thought . . . Alex said you'd gone.'

'Yes,' Jake said. 'I went to the hospital but I was coming back.'

'I — I thought you were mad at me?'

His face softened. He moved his hand from her arm to her face and stroked her cheek.

'Oh, Becky, my love, why would I be mad at you? I love you.'

'But I thought . . . I thought you wanted . . .'

'I want you,' he said. 'I love you. Don't you know that yet? I'm crazy about you, Becky. I've been keeping my distance, giving you space and time, hoping that in time you'd feel the same. All I want, all I've ever wanted is your love.'

Becky's mouth was dry. Her heart was pounding, thumping, crashing against her ribs.

'I've always loved you, Jake,' she said at last.

'You mean that?' he said huskily. 'I wasn't just a shoulder to cry on?'

'You were never just that,' she murmured. 'Oh, Jake, if you knew how much I loved you.'

'I'm beginning to get an idea,' he said.

He took her into his arms and kissed her.

Becky's heart soared inside her.

She nestled into his arms. Moments ago she'd been horrified at how close their seats were on the plane. Now she was wishing they were closer. She didn't want to be apart from him again — ever.

'Marry me, Becky,' he said, impulsively, overcome with joy and relief.

A stewardess approached them.

'Excuse me,' she said. 'You two obviously know each other . . .'

Jake and Becky laughed, arms still entwined around each other.

'There are two empty seats at the front . . . they're available if you'd like to sit together?'

'Yes,' Becky said. 'Yes to the seats and yes to you, Jake.'

'We won't be parted again,' Jake vowed and Becky leaned against him, his arm winding round her as he kissed the top of her head. 'This is where you belong. With me. Forever.'

And she settled into his arms, head resting against him, listening to the steady beating of his heart, closing her eyes not to close anything out, but to close her happiness in.

Forever.

THE END

We do hope that you have enjoyed reading this large print book.

Did you know that all of our titles are available for purchase?

We publish a wide range of high quality large print books including:
Romances, Mysteries, Classics
General Fiction
Non Fiction and Westerns

Special interest titles available in large print are:
The Little Oxford Dictionary
Music Book, Song Book
Hymn Book, Service Book

Also available from us courtesy of Oxford University Press:
Young Readers' Dictionary
(large print edition)
Young Readers' Thesaurus
(large print edition)

For further information or a free brochure, please contact us at:
Ulverscroft Large Print Books Ltd.,
The Green, Bradgate Road, Anstey,
Leicester, LE7 7FU, England.
Tel: (00 44) **0116 236 4325**
Fax: (00 44) **0116 234 0205**

WAITING FOR A
STAR TO FALL

Wendy Kremer

Lucy and Ethan grew up together. Lucy worshipped Ethan from afar and was disenchanted when he left for university, and didn't return. She hadn't realised that this was because of his family's hidden problems. Lucy is now the village librarian and Ethan is a well-known author. When Ethan comes back to the village and into her life again, can he shed his obsession with the past? Will they master the obstacles and find each other before it's too late?

LADY CHARLOTTE'S SECRET

Fenella Miller

Determined to fulfil her promise to a friend, Charlotte defies her brother and sets out on a journey in secret. But the person most at risk is herself, as circumstances conspire to leave her helpless in the care of a stranger. Dr James Hunter is a modern man, dedicating his life to aristocracy. When he discovers Charlotte's secret will it destroy their love?

SNOWBOUND

Fay Cunningham

When Amy agrees to help famous cosmetic surgeon Ethan Stopes write his memoirs, she is expecting a few quiet days in the country. Instead she spends an eventful Christmas trapped in a lonely manor with Ethan, his ex-wife, and his two children — and falls in love . . . Amy discovers Ethan's secret, and passions flare as the snow deepens. Somehow, she must help the enigmatic surgeon finish his book before it is too late . . .

THE BLACKSMITH'S DAUGHTER

Roberta Grieve

Tilly Masters hopes to follow in her father's footsteps as the village blacksmith and is upset when he takes on an assistant. But she falls in love with Nathan and is devastated when he enlists and is sent to France. She vows to wait for him but her aunt has other ambitions for her — marriage to the local squire's son. Will Tilly succumb to his advances or cling to the hope that Nathan will return from the war?

SECRETS OF THE PAST

Sheila Lewis

When Anne Osmond disappears, Romy Haldane is suspected of being the last person she'd had contact with, although they'd never met. Romy offers to help Matt, Anne's employer, to search for her. Unexpectedly, their investigations prompt some long hidden memories for Romy — as well as warm feelings towards Matt. Earlier, Anne had embarked upon a personal quest which uncovered disturbing secrets from the past, and recorded them in her diary — secrets which now hold the key to her whereabouts . . .